THE SWALLOWED TOWN

[& OTHER RABBIT HOLES YOU SHOULD AVOID]

A NOVEL

THE SWALLOWED TOWN

C. F. PAGE

This is a work of fiction. The characters, places, and situations are either the product of the author's imagination or are used fictitiously. Any resemblance to actual persons, living or dead, events, or locales is entirely coincidental.

THE SWALLOWED TOWN

Copyright © 2026 by C. F. Page

All rights reserved.

"Got a light?" is a quote from *Twin Peaks: The Return*, created by David Lynch and Mark Frost. Used with acknowledgment. All other quotes used are public domain.

Published by Truborn Press

Edited by William Sterling

Cover Art by Matt Seff Barnes

Cover Design by Truborn Design

ISBN: 979-8-9915969-8-5 (paperback)
ISBN: 979-8-9915969-9-2 (ebook)

FIRST EDITION: 2026

10 9 8 7 6 5 4 3 2 1

For Jordan Peele, Justin Benson,
Alex Garland, David Lynch,
Michael Wehunt, John Langan,
Laird Barron, Matt Cardin, H.P.
Lovecraft, Thomas Ligotti, Hidetaka
Miyazaki, Damon Lindelof, Nic
Pizzolatto, Sam Lake, and Jeff
VanderMeer

but mostly for Angie

darkest places from our collective waterlogged night-mares. You're going to love this bleak read!"

—Corey Farrenkopf,
author of *Living in Cemeteries* and *Haunted Ecologies*

"Page creates an unsettling **Lovecraftian mystery** that on its own will terrify, but he adds to the horror by having it unfold in our conspiracy-drenched modern world. This book crawls under your skin and nests there."

—Elford Alley,
author of *Apartment 239* and *Never Leaving*

"Bold, verbose, and with a style that's equally hallucinogenic and **idiosyncratic**, Page's *The Swallowed Town* is a multi-layered coastal horror nightmare."

—Richard Beauchamp,
author of *Thrall* and *Devil Makes Three*

"Intricately designed and aesthetically ominous. Brooding and mystical. *The Southern Reach Trilogy* meets *House of Leaves* meets *The Lighthouse*."

—Charlotte Dune,
author of *Acid Christmas*

"*The Swallowed Town* is one of those stories that, despite making you uncomfortable, wraps its tentacles around you and pulls you in. It lovingly presses its deceptively sharp claws into your mind and doesn't let go. **Page is at his uncompromising best here**, sinking you into a nightmare you're far too invested in to ever want to wake up from."

—Tobin Elliott,
author of the six-book horror series *The Aphotic*

Praise for

ORPHANS OF THE ATERCOSM

"Page's writing is much like Lovecraft's oceans: glassy smooth in places, terrifyingly brutal in others, ever dark and full of mystery. *Atercosm* seduces with its eerie wonders and horrifies with its glimpses beyond the veil, where fathomless revelations linger just beyond our comprehension. Those who read this collection will encounter Page's **unique brand of literary madness**."

—Felix Blackwell,
bestselling author of *Stolen Tongues*

"**A tour de force of the weird** and the uncanny, C.F. Page's *Orphans of the Atercosm* is a must read for fans of Ligotti, Lovecraft, and all things weird horror."

—Richard Beauchamp,
author of *Black Tongue & Other Anomalies*

"C.F. Page is a **unique and gifted storyteller**, and he's accomplished what very few authors have for me: aside from the fascinating story and interesting characters, Page manages to pull me back in through a unique and incredible writing style that I simply could not get enough of."

—Tobin Elliott,
author of the six-book horror series, *The Aphotic*

"*Orphans of the Atercosm* is a powerful reminder of why we must write horror. Page has a **skillful mastery of structure and language**, tormenting the reader the same way he torments his characters. This is a dark, cyclical exploration of the recesses of Page's mind, and the descent into his depravity is well worth it."

—Aaron Beardsell,
author of *Dead Station* and *Coffinwood*

Praise for

NATIVE FEAR

"It's a **beautiful, brutal, complex, terrifying** read" (five stars).

—*Scream Magazine*

"Page's *Native Fear* is a blistering and evocative examination of man's darkness. **A harrowing read**."

—Steve Stred,

Splatterpunk-nominated author of Sacrament and

Mastodon

"Debut author [C. F.] Page presents an intricate horror novel . . . an inventive take on a rural place filled with unspeakable malice."

—Kirkus Reviews

(SIDE B)

THE DARKHOUSE

"Got a light?"
—**The Woodsman, *Twin Peaks***

"Never explain anything."
—**H. P. Lovecraft**

Last Letter

If you're reading this, then I'm either dead or some semantical variation of "dead"—e.g., insane beyond rehabilitant expectations, literally not part of this world (but not necessarily dead-dead: I'll get to that later), or I may just . . . not necessarily be "me" anymore.

My laptop password is ▮▮▮▮▮▮▮▮. You'll find everything in a folder called ▮▮▮▮▮▮▮▮▮▮▮▮▮▮▮▮▮▮▮. I'm sure you'd have figured it out anyway, considering all of our sessions together. In this folder you'll find transcripts, audio and video files, <u>everything</u>—all pertaining to the town we've discussed, the job I took, the article I wrote, and the nightmares still plaguing me . . . of the ~~light~~ darkhouse and what resides in its bowels.

But I still need to know what the number means; I need to see if it works.

If this seems cryptic, I'm sorry.

Everything will make sense ▮▮▮▮▮▮▮▮.

-FT

IN THE LATER MONTHS OF autumn, on the coast of the southern regional town of ████████ (its exact whereabouts are undisclosed for reasons that will become clearer), the blackly foaming tides bring about what the inhabitants of the coastal town call *Sea Manna*. Annually, these *Sea Manna* wash ashore for a day or two—sometimes for up to a week—and never before 3 AM nor after 5 AM: the uncomfortable coincidence with the Devil's Hour may be nothing more than happenstance.

I learned all of this in very small print from a pamphlet I had stepped on during my morning jog on my second day in town. On the bottom of the pamphlet were directions to the Museum of the Fish (TO LEARN MORE!), which, stated in even *finer* print, "has been an accumulative and collective effort by volunteer native historians, academics, and devotees to chronicle, consolidate, and showcase the history of the *Sea Manna*'s nebulous, esoteric, and religious origins," and to try their best to "extract fact"—or near enough fact—"from mythology."

I should, however, tell you that I came to this quaint and rustic, sea-breeze-corroded and sun-beaten town for a reason dissociated from this annual marine phenomenon and its coinciding festival. I arrived in winter—

well beyond the *Sea Manna* timeframe. In fact, I was quite dismayed to have missed it—the *Sea Manna*, that is, not the festival itself; I tend to abstain from social gatherings as a general rule, hence my chosen profession.

After completing my morning jog, I visited the museum.

When I asked the volunteer—an old Native American sporting an argyle flat cap, one a younger man wouldn't have been capable of authentically "pulling off"—what the *Sea Manna* were, he sort of looked at me funny. His expression gave me gooseflesh. "It's the flesh of the fish," he said.

"What kind of fish?"

"*The* fish." And I thought that that was all he was going to say before he drew in a breath that sounded like a boiling kettle. He rolled his eyes ever so faintly (as if I should have *known*) and concluded with: "The fish that swallowed Jonah."

I admit—my church days being little more than a distant memory of my youth—I didn't immediately follow the logic. Then I happened to glance at an elegant mural on the wall (dated 1975) and saw either a whale or a big fish. There was a praying man in its belly, visible via some x-ray vision the artist had given to the observer; and, in the sky above, what looked to be a disproportionately titanic being of seraphic properties[1]—it was bone-white and lustrous, with absurdly wide, profound wings.

"Oh, *that* fish."

---

[1] Sitting at this chintzy ███████ Motel desk, writing down this macabre account, I admit to you that on deeper reflection I might even say "demonic."

"That fish," the volunteer said again, and then he added something that has unsettled my psyche ever since . . . although I can't quite place a finger on the reason *why*, let alone recall to you any one word or sentence or facial gesture that has caused such psychic *distress*, except to articulate—although perhaps not very well—that it was an amalgam of these things:

- his gravelly voice
- the almost wolfish quality of the howling wind
- the sounds of distant but violent rock-smashing waves
- the screaming-bloody-murder seagulls
- the odd elevator music playing through unseen speakers (odd because of how blank the walls were, which has given me an absurd number of sleepless nights since—squirming around in bed, my mind racing, my disembodied consciousness zigging and zagging about the ceiling of the Museum, searching for those speakers)
- my already elevated heartrate from my morning jog
- and, finally, the uncanny history of the town itself

This unholy planetary alignment of details had left behind, in an alcove of my subconscious, some *modus* of psychic fungal growth imbued with mountainous melancholy and allusive trepidation.

"The year was 1650," he began, "when a large group of about three families, due to allegations of witchcraft, had found themselves banished from their village. Mind you, this was four decades *before* the popularized Salem witch trials, but the pre-American colonists of that period had carried with them this anxiety—no, *mania*—from Europe, whose witch-hunts had already begun a century earlier and whose death toll so greatly squashed Salem's it makes you wonder why that town's tragedy ever reached such mainstream appeal. But I digress.

"Anyways, the village elders cast them away without so much as a chicken, let alone a loaf of bread, perhaps thinking the excommunicated families would use the livestock for Satanic rituals; but that's just my own tongue running. Point being, they were hungry.

"For weeks they'd went south because it had been autumn already; warmer weather was preferable as the ever-creeping winter approached—especially since they had a whole slew of kids and at least two babies. But they'd gone south until they could go south no further, arriving at the very sea you hear right now through these walls . . .

"You already see the statue in the downtown area?"

"Of the two men and the woman around what looks like a campfire?" I said.

"That's the one," he said.

"Then I suppose that means I've seen it."

He walked toward the window to show me something, and I followed to see the thing he were to show. Once there, he nodded for me to look out the pane of glass. I did, but had to crane my neck and squint really hard to even see the statue's mere glimmers beyond a few too-close and wide-branched yaupons whose fiercely flapping leaves appeared like thousands of shaking maracas. "That's Henry O'Connor, Fredrick Grayson, and Margaret Radon, whom our town considers its founding fathers *and* mother."

"Why them?" I asked.

The volunteer stared at me blankly for a moment, then hummed, then, with a somnambulant motion, rubbed his chin, then hummed some more. "Well. Could be they just left behind more journals than the others, which made us believe they were more important."

He shrugged and hummed again, his gaze drifting to a place between the top of my head and the Museum's ceiling for a moment before he restored his narrative impetus with a taut shake of his head.

"As I was *saying*. That statue beyond the trees represents the first night of their Great Fast."

"*Great* Fast?"

"Well, they had no weapons to hunt with. And I reckon you may not know that the American Indians 'round here—probably my ancestors—had been a, let's say, *peculiar folk*. Won't find them in the histories—at least not the mainstream ones, no sir. My ancestors were not brutal, per se, as were the Kiowa and Apache back then, but they were inhospitable just the same. Some local historians say they were a 'fringe-tribe'—whatever *that* means."

A silence suddenly grew between us, wherein a shadow swam through it and molded shark-like features onto the volunteer's face—whatever *that* means.

"Then there was the whole communication barrier, too, so they never attempted—never *risked*—asking the tribe for food . . .

"*Anyways*. Soon after stumbling upon this land, this town's founders picked themselves a spot on the beach, set up a measly camp, and they waited."

"For what?" I imagined the taste of sea on my tongue and a harrow of wolves wailing against the pane of time-worn glass through which I stared.

"Either for a merciful end. Or a great miracle. What else would there have been?"

"They could have eaten plants," I said.

"Coulda, sure," he said. "And they *did*. Got real sick real fast and died. Bad luck or bad vegetation or bad juju, who's to say. In their journals they mentioned the plants and the animals '*being cursed with black rot,*' if you can believe that."

I couldn't, but said nothing of it.

"Let me guess," I then said. "This was when they discovered the . . . um, *Sea Manna,* when God fed them like the Israelites in the desert." I felt proud to have deduced this conclusion all by myself; more impressive still because of how very little of the Bible I knew.

The volunteer turned and smiled.

"Not exactly. After a few weeks of deliberate or *undeliberate* fasting, during which at least three of the elders and one of the babies passed away—although some accounts imply *all* the babies died—they saw, all of them—and you can read the digitally transferred journal entries on those computers, each from different accounts—what at least five of them call a GREAT DOVE; three accounts describe a Lordly archangel with immense wings; and one of them—Henry O'Connor's cousin from his mother's side, a certain Charlie Blackwood—said it was God's *literal* hand, '. . . *only,*' and I quote, '*HE must have been wearing a glove so as to avoid our losing our sanities in seeing HIS Holy flesh, but the superwhite radiance bled through the great fabric nonetheless.*' And what's more, Blackwood was an atheist prior to this; the spectacle he'd seen—and you can cross-reference this bold claim with at least four journals if this seems preposterous—well, it had *immediately* converted him."

I wanted to point out that people throughout human history had come to religion (or belief in the supernatural) for less spectacular reasons, but held my tongue; I didn't think I would have been able to insert myself into his wall of well-rehearsed words even if I'd tried.

"And speaking of Blackwood," he continued. "It was

his wife who was the reason for their being tainted with witchcraft accusations in the first place, which you can read about in Margaret Radon's journal.

"The severity of casting three whole families into the wilderness aside, Alma Rowling[2] actually did seem to do witchcraft of some variety, to some degree, although we don't have too many examples aside from what Radon indicated: that in their previous village someone's dog had been beheaded, its tongue and liver cast into a hot skillet over a fire and left there for all the townsfolk to see the next morning—some pagan symbol had been blade-etched into its skull, red roses skewered into its hollowed-out eyes. Radon had only *speculated* it was Alma; but it confirms as much if you read Henry's journal—though he seemed even *more* furious with his then-atheist cousin Charlie, who, as he put it, married 'such a witch.'

"But I ramble."

He turned away from the window and motioned for me to follow him to a few oddments behind cases. There were outfits, letters, tools, a wagon wheel; there were bones, guns, daggers; vases and pots and pans and utensils; tattered books, tattered boots, tattered dreams; and ("what's that?" I asked, to which he replied "one of *their* skeletons," before continuing with his original train of thought) what looked like an off-putting, too-symmetrical tumbleweed.

"My point is this: Charlie Blackwood founded the Church of the Fish, wrote *The Second Book of Jonah*, became the High Vicar (what you'd call a *pastor* or

---

[2] I remember an outbreak of gooseflesh, and I'd zeroed in on his words. The name "Rowling" was the reason I was in ███████ to begin with.

priest), assembled the School of Yahweh ('school' as in 'school of fish'—*deacons,* basically), and just this one event caused him to transition from a witch-married atheist to religious leader. It's said he even built the church himself, with his own hands and no help whatsoever. The church is at the end of the road from where the lighthouse is. You must've seen it. Rumor has it that Charlie Blackwood built that, too—the lighthouse, I mean—or at least he heavily oversaw its construction. It was meant as a tokenish homage to the Fish whose flesh nourished their bodies, whose flesh—at least from Charlie's point of view—attributed to nourishing his *un*body, too. His immortal spirit."

My heart started to flutter at the mention of the lighthouse (you will understand shortly as to why), but, for better or for worse, I still had to gather some details on the *Manna* for my own sensibilities.

"So what does the 'great dove' and Jonah's fish—or whale or whatever—have to do with the *Sea Manna?*" I asked. "Did it fly over them sprinkling down those little fishy globsters? What I'm assuming *actually* happened," said I, a skeptic of all things cosmic, supernatural, and divine, "is that they saw a cloud over the ocean. Maybe it looked like it had wings. And maybe they were all exhausted and starved. And maybe sometime later the shore was full of these . . . native organisms. The pilgrim outcasts just got lucky with their timing was all—these things had probably washed ashore many times before their being there."

He looked at me evenly.

"I must have missed the part about the GREAT DOVE having clawed about the ocean and raised into the sky a great black whale from the unfathomable depths of Hell; and the part where, with its talons—or HIS fingers, if you consider Charlie's interpretation—it dug into the whale's gut and spewed into the ocean its fishy innards." Now glancing at his watch, he seemed to grow edgy. But he continued nonetheless:

"But you are right about one thing: it wasn't long before the Fish's 'blessed flesh' washed ashore for them to consume. And consider their shared horror *until* the *Sea Manna* came. Consider what went through their heads. In the Bible, when an angel—which technically means 'messenger,' 'angel' describing what it *does*, not what it *is*—well, when one appears, it always says something along the lines of 'Be not afraid.' But if this had been an angel, it forgot to tell them that. It—he—*whatever*—let them fester in horror for probably a great many hours as they stood on the beach in awe of what they'd just seen."

"The *Sea Manna* is obviously just an organism, not whale flesh," I verbally jousted, finding the whole fantastical story to be as farcical as it was compelling; but the volunteer countered with—

"I don't think any of them knew what whale flesh looked like." The volunteer sighed and looked around the small museum with weary, red-rimmed gray eyes, and then glanced at his watch. "That's how the story goes, anyways, but I really must get going—smoke break."

"Just two more questions."

He cocked his head, studying me as if exploring my eyes and the structure of my face could somehow tell him the ease in which he could answer my pending questions. He sighed heavily and I thought I got a whiff of sulfur and brine—which made me think of dead fish rotting on a beach—but it dissipated almost immediately.

He said, "Fire away."

"Well, haven't marine biologists studied the *Sea Manna*?"

The old Native American shrugged. "*Maybe.* But it's not like anybody *wants* to debunk it, understand? What's the word for those types? Trolls; yeah, *them*; we don't have *them* here. The tradition of the Festival is important for ██████. Hell, *I* don't believe the *Sea Manna* is the literal flesh from the same exact whale that swallowed Jonah—I doubt that ever even happened. No offense, if you're a believer." He laughed. "But just because *I* don't believe it doesn't mean I think a little bit of fantasy isn't good for our local culture. Our community."

He pulled out a pack of Marlboros, tapped the bottom until a filter poked out its tawny head, and stood there contemplating.

"*Community.*

"Think about that, will you? That word. People with *common* values who are in *unity*. What's so bad about that? Who cares if they sprinkle a bit of fairy dust over their—*our*—culture?

"All I know is that—miraculously divine or naturalistically coincidental—the flesh of Jonah's *Fish* or just some strange marine organisms—this town owes its very establishment to the, as you called them, 'fishy globsters'; the town would *not* have endured throughout the ages without the Church; and the economy—the town—would *not* have survived without the tourism brought by the Festival." And after pulling out the cigarette and stuffing the pack back into his pocket, he made his way toward the ocean-facing side door. Just before he left, he turned and said something that wouldn't make sense until much later. "My advice to you, son: don't linger here for longer than you have to, and stay away from dark, damp places."

My one last question—about what the local newspapers called the Lighthouse Killings, which was the whole reason I was in ██████████ in the first place—violently disintegrated as I stood there, manically dissecting his portentous and baffling last words. (The next time I saw this man, a third eye—weeping redly—stared back at me.)

Then I got a text from the contact I'd procured the previous night at a bar called *The Fish Tavern*, a woman with some local government ins and outs.

THE LIGHTHOUSE KEY IS UNDER pink rock.

U have 5 hours before u need 2 leave crime
scene.

They come like clockwork after 7.

Found Footage

HANDHELD AND SHAKY, *the camera focuses on the front porch, capturing the weather-beaten door at its center. Engraved banisters flank five weed-choked stone steps. Despite the daylight, the footage appears grainy and aged. An antediluvian skeleton key emerges into view, gripped between thumb and forefinger knuckle, and, as we ascend the stairs, the cameraman says, "Per your request, Mr. Maxwell, everything will be documented. As you can see, I'm attempting to open the door. Hopefully the key works. And—wait—hold on—there it goes."*

The hinge shrieks as the door swings inward.

We see a small mudroom, cataleptic save for the lazily drifting dust motes seen in boles of muted sunlight cutting in from the curtained-off windows on either side of the door, which opens via pocket door into the vestibule. A hand comes into frame and pushes the door all the way into its pocket.

Thickly dusted hardwood floors tap tap tap as we move forward.

The vestibule is bare and dusty, small and low-ceilinged, and branching off in either direction; and we, passengers of the footage, go rightward ("looks like the other way is a little office or something—I'll have to swing through on the way back"), where there's a short hallway lined with framed photographs of blank-faced somnam-bulists, their expressions those of porcelain; paintings of sepulchral, lonely rural landscapes, decaying husks of some faraway, impalpable humanness; and in a spot where a large painting had clearly been taken down—a big horizontal rectangle in its absence, blackened with grime and dense dust at its edges—is the spray-painted gibberish:

And dissonantly encircling the enigmatic words are a batch of wooden crucifixes whose wood-carved occupants are not the thorn-crowned, spear-penetrated Jesus of Nazareth—instead they are fish, gaudily painted as if by children. Twine-bound.

"This is the first time I've seen these," says our cameraman.

Swaying side to side, we traverse the hallway and stop where it angles again leftward: into what room, we cannot yet see. Just barely enough light bends down the corridor from the vestibule. Somewhere a chainsaw revs up—no, just heavy breathing (from the cameraman, of course). "This is where, allegedly"— clearing his throat— "the mother of the, um, young man. Where the police found only a part of her. What kind of sick fuck cuts off his mother's head and draws a fish underneath—and a male . . . appendage going into the fish's mouth? If I'd been one of the responding officers, I don't think I'd've handcuffed him, Mr. Maxwell. If you catch my drift. But then I wouldn't have this job, right? Holy Hell . . ."

The world jitters as we lower with the cameraman. A hand comes into frame. His other hand. Left hand. We hear sounds like nails on a chalkboard as he first rubs at a spot on the wood floor, and then scratches it. "Is that . . . ?" But he doesn't share what he thinks "that" might be; and via the graininess of picture, and the camera not thriving in low light, we can only speculate whether it's a blotch of old blood or the chalky remains of a fish . . . or phallus.

Up.

Camera at eye level now.

We turn left.

A long-abandoned living quarters. A stairwell coils upward around the spacious room, leading to the access of the lighthouse itself. What is probably yellow light, but what looks green via quality of footage, creeps in through grime-caked windows whose moldering, arachnid-infested entrails lay about the floor—i.e., great gothic curtains, the color of which may have once been burgundy, but the footage makes them look like strange black sea matter. About the ceiling fan blades hang things from small threads too pixelated to identify. Despite the light washing over the room—albeit, not much—it's somehow still too murky to identify anything in great detail. Perhaps (if one has propensities toward the supernatural) the dark is the incorporeal residue of the familicidal crimes committed.

"This is where it happened. Most of it, anyway. Except for the condemned's father, whose death and, um . . . post-mortem bodily amendments occurred up

there"—camera tilts up, a spiral motion to show the trajectory of the stairwell—"in the lantern room. Which brings me to the reason for my being here, as well as this investigation. I think Truman Capote would have killed for this story."

We walk deeper into the room.

Milky distortion.

Something hisses—electronically, not organically.

And we remain in this grainy video-recording limbo as the cameraman talks about the Lighthouse Killings; relays to us certain details extracted from interviews he's thus far conducted, about how Hector Rowling's father and his father's father and his father's father's father, and so on, had all been what the locals refer to—and not without a discernible measure of reverence—the [Lighthouse] Keepers, "almost as if," he's saying, "it meant something more than just the obvious," although . . .

"*. . . WHEN HE WAS YOUNGER, Titus—that's the infamous Hector's father, as well as my best friend—well, he was my best friend. Was, of course, 'cause I don't keep company with the dead—well, he didn't actually want to be the Keeper; in fact, his older brother Bill had been set to be the Keeper since that was custom among the Rowlings' heritage and was also in keeping with the rituals of the Church. You know, the oldest son and all that—very traditional family they were. Even though Bill . . . well, this ain't hush-hush considering it was in the news when he died and, besides, everyone in ▮▮▮▮ ▮▮▮ knew even before the news broke. Where was I? Oh. For some reason I'm beating around the bush, but I guess I'll just say it: Bill was a drug addict. Died of an OD in '75 I think it was. But despite that—the addiction, not the death—their father, Gabriel—although I always called him Mr. Rowling because it sounds weird using his Christian name so informally—well, he still expected Bill to conserve the tradition. Although that word—'tradition'—sounds too casual, too unceremonious, if that makes sense . . . maybe it doesn't . . . anyway, let me explain: With the Rowlings—I guess with us ▮▮▮▮▮▮-folk, too, especially those of us in the Church—it has a deeper kind of meaning. Very deep. Almost like the Royal*

Family. So deep a meaning that it's dark—but not light-less. It's as if Mr. Rowling—Gabriel—believed Bill would rise to the responsibility because of that nameless, trans-cendent, somewhat metaphysical word; who knows. Maybe if Bill hadn't injected a little too much of that poison into his veins on that unfortunate day in November (I remember because it was one day after the Sea Manna had washed ashore and the day before the Festival began), then he would have risen to the occasion. But I believe it was a suicide."

"How so?"

"Well. For two reasons. Maybe two and a half rea-sons. Or more. Maybe an infinite number of reasons. But I'll stick with the two reasons—and maybe the half-reason if it fits organically into how my tongue pulls out this yarn."

"I could always ask you what that 'half-reason' is afterward, if you happen not to fit it in, as you say, 'organica—'"

"—doesn't work like that, fella. The half-reason is something you feel; can't just . . . say it; you have to convey it in a roundabout way or not at all."

"Okay, then I won't press the issue. What are the two—and possibly the 'half'—reasons you believe Bill Rowling committed suicide by drugs rather than acci-dentally ODing? And what does this have to do with Bill's nephew, Hector, having killed—or having been con-demned for killing—his family? Do you think there was sufficient evidence?"

"You're asking too many questions; but understand-ing the mystery of Bill's suicide will inadvertently answer the latter questions about Hector and the Lighthouse Killings, if only you'll stop and listen. Are you still recording this?"

"Yessir."

"I'd rather you not, Mr. Journalist. Not from this point on. If this got back to Father Shachor, well, I wouldn't want that."

"Who's Father Shachor?"

No response.

A rustling of fabric.

A metal hinge squealing.

"Would you like me to continue recording this in shorthand?"

"I'd rather you commit it to memory, if it's all the same." A mumble.[3] *"I—just, you know, just in case someone gets a hold of your . . . whatever your recording gizmo is— shhh. Hear that?"*

"Wind and waves are all I hear. Some seagulls, too."

"SHHH! Listen. Can you look out my window?"

A long beat.

"Well, can you?"

"Yes."

Footfalls.

"You looking?"

"I'm looking."

"See a black van?"

"Why?"

"Do you?"

"I don't."

"Look out that other window, too."

Footfalls.

"I'm looking. No black van, sedan, truck, hearse, clown car, or limo. Any other windows you want me to check?"

A long beat.

"Kitchen window. Around the corner."

---

[3] After enhancing the audio: "although maybe even that's not beyond Father Shachor's reach."

A noise (likely a sigh).

A fumbling and clatter of dishes and a hushed curse.

A faint, distorted voice: "Nothing."

"Go upstairs and check the windows—"

"I can assure *you, Mr. Esko, from just looking out these windows, that there is no black—"*

"I don't want you to look out the windows; I want you to check if they're closed and locked."

Footfalls reverberate, get louder.

"It's through that door right there. Yep. That one. Give it a tug; the door doesn't sit properly in the frame; this house is two hundred years old, and—what with the wind, rain, and relentless sun, not to mention God knows what else the ocean brings about from its depths on those strange, star-stained nights—it settled in funny ways. I swear some rooms are smaller than they once were, other rooms larger, floorboards creak differently (sometimes a crackle, sometimes a moan), and water stains migrate from room to room . . . I'm rambling. Don't mind the clutter on the stairwell. I don't want no lawsuit, neither; you came here to ask your questions, Mr. Journalist, and I'm answering—so don't be tripping and breaking any bones now. I would go up there myself but, as you can see, I don't have any goddamn legs—the 'betes took 'em—so if you wouldn't mind just easing an old man's worries."

"Fine. Give me a sec."

Footfalls.

Shuffling and thudding.

The squealing of a hinge; the grinding of something against something; a muffled voice.

"Say again?"

Voice indiscernible.[4]
Raised voice: "There's another window in the bath-room."
A beat.
A scream.
Coughing.
Gagging.
Static.
A low wind
(conchlike).
A clatter.
End of file.

---

[4] Audio enhanced: "Why are you concerned about a black van?"

"FELIX SPEAKING," I said as I climbed into my Chevy pickup, the phone wedged between my shoulder and ear. It had vibrated a moment earlier, and I'd be lying if I said the sheer unexpectedness of it hadn't nearly evacuated my bowels. This was after my jog back to the motel from the museum and a lightning-quick shower—all the while echoey elevator music playing in my head, a windswept score disseminating the volunteer's ominous warning about dark and damp places.

"*Felix, it's Maxwell,*" said Maxwell—which I already knew because of the caller ID.

"Nice to finally talk to you on the phone," I said. "Expected you'd sound different."

A noncommittal chuckle.

"Hey, um, I'm about to head to the lighthouse. I've got access for five—"

He cut me off: "*I'm calling because . . . well, I haven't been* completely *honest about a certain detail . . .*"

"What detail?"

"*I can't say over the phone. And even if I could, it's something I have to show you. I'll text you my address. You'll be compensated for your time, of course, don't worry, considering this particular . . .* development.

What I have to tell you—show you, I mean—won't take long, and I would have told you—shown you—this earlier, except this information wasn't provided to me until about ten minutes ago. And Felix? I must ask something. Please don't let this question alarm you—it's only a precaution—but do you carry a gun?"

THE HOUSE, which stood in an amalgam of wood and swamp five miles outside town, was much smaller than I expected from a man who'd so casually paid $25,000 to a scarcely published journalist. I pulled into the driveway and got out and stretched my legs, surprised by how tranquil his property was.

How *modest.*

There was a 2013 Chrysler Pacifica: a dent in its side, evidence of rust around the rims, not even parked in the garage for protection against the elements—which I realized, as I looked into the garage, was because boxed and tarp-wrapped goods were spilling out of it (albeit of an organized hand, and far from what I'd consider hoarder-ish); a lawn that hadn't felt a blade in weeks, dead twigs haphazardly scattered across the yard, and a house—very old and probably less than 3,000 square feet—in dire need of treatment. I say "treatment" rather than "fresh coat of paint" perhaps because the blotchy, peeling-away portions seemed like evidence of a decaying disease. Corporeal and somehow *un*metaphorical. It was as if I had tapped into some kind of psychic ore, and the feeling I felt—the one that made me think I was traversing into some kind of contaminated head pretending to be a house, with a mouth pretending to be a door—was telling me to get out of Dodge. (I obviously should have listened, considering what happened—what is *still* happening.)

My jeans flapped against the wind as I made my way up the stone path branching off the driveway. Gargoylish sculptures and birdbaths on either side kept me in line, leading me to the front porch. There were six stone steps, wide and cracked, with greenish-gray matter pushing through the gaps.

As I reached the final step, a branch snapped somewhere in the distance. For some reason I felt compelled to turn. Long I peered into a peculiar shadow cast by a tree at the fringe of forest partially enclosing Maxwell's property. In my mind's eye I saw a woman standing in that shadow . . . staring at me with huge, milky eyes—a rotten, bloated, *blackened* thing—but of course it was only my nerve-jangled imagination hewing horror from the mundane—

The

(*mouth*)

door yawned open with a whiny rust-embedded squeal and I almost screamed.

"Come in," said a rather short silhouette, which clashed harshly with his deep voice (I expected a taller man), as he stepped into a sliver of bleeding-in daylight.

I turned back around because I thought I'd heard a woman say something—just one word—somewhere behind me ("Charles," might have been that one word), maybe from the spot where the thing-I-had-only-imagined had been, but it must've been the wind . . .

EVERYTHING ABOUT MAXWELL SEEMED MODEST—from his car to his property to his blue jeans and burgundy Adidas sweater a decade out of fashion—so it came as no surprise that his foyer was modest, too (HOME SWEET HOME on the door mat, probably bought from Walmart), which led to a modest living room. The hardwood floor, modest of course, had lost its original gloss: now dull and pocked and scratched and stained, and there seemed to have been an attempt in a distant past where rugs—albeit mismatched and rather chintzy and, yes, the *m-word*—were haphazardly strewn about to hide the worst of the imperfections. Some rugs now slept near the walls like dusty, malodourous scrolls meant for the hands of giants.

Reading my thoughts: "Don't mind the neglect. Nor the *mundanity of things*. My wife . . ." He raised a hand to show a gold band around his ring finger. "She passed away how long ago? Has it already been ten years? Anyway. Follow me and watch your step. And, um, yes, nice to meet you. I'd shake hands with you, Mr. Trellis, but, well, forgive me, but I guess you might call a certain psychological disposition I have *germaphobia*. Though the scientific name is *Mysophobia*. I've had it since childhood. It's nothing personal. I, um, yeah—

"Just up the stairs."

"I like the exposed brick," I said by way of making small talk. "It gives the house character."

He turned and said, "Exposed what?" Then he saw and said, "Yes, that. Exposed brick. Of course, yes, character, mhmm." Then he made a sound—something like a bark, but was probably a laugh. "*Character*: it certainly has that."

The stairwell hugged the wall until we came to a small landing. A window showcased a weed- and tall grass-strangled backyard. An abandoned beehive dangled from an arm of a low-hanging Oak, hoary mold infecting both branch and hive like the kiss of a light snowfall. Underneath this unwell Oak dangled a moveless kids' swing; I almost asked if he had a child, but the landing moaned underfoot as he ascended the last stretch of stairs.

Maxwell briefly disappeared from my sightline when he turned left. A door creaked open. Absconding foot-falls. A *click* of a switch and an orange-yellow glow flooded the otherwise dim hallway. And my feet found the top floor and I turned the corner. Up here, Maxwell didn't bother using a rug to hide the unpleasant scuffs, deep gouges, or abhorrent stains about the stretch of floor. There was no decor except for a grandiose grandfa-ther clock at the very end of the hallway, its hands stuck at 11:50. Minutes to midnight. I shivered.

"Have a seat, Mr. Trellis."

I made my way into the first room on the left. If everything else about Maxwell was modest, his office was everything but. A tall, elegant bookshelf lined one wall, the tomes all hardcover, without sleeves, and very, very old; to the bookshelf's right, between two windows, a liquor cabinet yawned open as Maxwell found a bottle of bourbon and picked up two clinking-together glasses; further rightward stood against the wall a behemoth wingback chair tucked into an antique desk that had scattered across its surface: books, journals, artifacts, coffee mugs, an old-timey lantern, and a huge monitor (I imagined it displayed a dozen or so surveillance feeds of the house and property)[5]; and in the corner—between desk and a wall jam-packed with paintings, giving way only to the doorway—was a vinyl record player.

I found the seat before the desk, opposite his own chair, and sat.

Maxwell presumptuously walked toward me with two glasses of sloshing bourbon and, extending one hand toward me, said, "Here," as if either I had asked for it or I *needed* it. I told him, "Thank you, Mr. Maxwell,

---

[5] Although in the end it didn't really help out Maxwell, did it?

but I'm fine."

His expression morphed. An image flashed through my mind of a kid who'd just dropped an ice cream cone. The glass shook in his hand as he looked around, as if he no longer knew what to do with it.

"What about coffee?"

"I like tea," I told him.

"Um, yes, I've got tea."

He poured the bourbon that'd been meant for me down his own gullet, exited his office ("just a moment," echoed his voice), and after a span of no more than three minutes I heard his moaning footfalls returning up the stairwell, *tap tap tapping* through the hallway, and, carrying his own glass of bourbon in one hand and my hot tea in the other, he handed me my tea before plopping down and sighing. He took one sip of his bourbon, then another, before saying, "You're not the first journalist I've hired for this task."

I didn't know what to say—I should have mentioned I liked my tea cold, not hot, but that ship had sailed so I took a sip out of courtesy. Then I registered his words' meaning and choked on the weirdly chalky, too-earthy tea; did he really just say—?

"Have you ever heard of a man named John R. Francis?"

Recovered from my short-lived paroxysm of coughs, I said, "I've heard the name," and set down the tea; when I did, however, he looked frantically at the mug. Then I saw the coaster to my right and set the mug upon it. Maxwell cleared his throat, looked at me, and said:

"He's had some work published in *GQ*, *Time*, and *Entertainment Weekly*—book reviews, mostly, from what I understand. And a couple of *Playboy* articles. He did a few online journals, too, and let me tell you this, Mr. Trellis: I investigated all he wrote and never found any—

what's the word?—*click-bait* articles; nor did he succumb to tilting his view on topics in allegiance to any ideology, even at the cost of his career. He was eventually fired—well . . . um, maybe I should say *societally ostracized*, yeah—for having the 'wrong' view on George Orwell's *1984*, for defending Abraham Lincoln, and for being an advocate of not altering dated books to match contemporary worldviews."

Maxwell shrugged, took another sip, repositioned himself in his behemoth wingback chair, scooted it closer to the desk, then scooted it farther away, then closer, then opened up a small notepad as if to jog his memory about what he was going to say next, then continued:

"We live in psychotic times, Mr. Trellis. Toxic times. Confused times. A thousand years from now we'll have the top historians look at this era and be very confused. Will they perhaps assume our national religion was Marvel?

"I digress.

"Francis had done a little bit of this, a little bit of that; I suppose he was your archetypical writer-for-hire. And his work ethic and his—*um*—his daringness, among other things, were what drew me in."

"And," said I, "your willingness to pay him a hefty sum at a time when he was blacklisted is what drew *him* in."

Unfolding and refolding his hands, he said, "Undoubtedly. But I told him what I told you—first half of payment is a retainer, so to speak, and the second half is when the job is done. Regardless of conclusion."

"Don't forget your mentioning of a bonus if I—*we*—could prove Hector's innocence."

"Of course, of course. Who could blame me? Besides, there needs to be incentive because if I'm right—

and I do believe I am—then to uncover the truth will be *most* challenging."

His eyes wandered to the window. Something tapped on it. A tree branch.

"So . . . *what*? You're willing to blow an extra twenty-five thousand and whoever gets to it first gets the second half? Was Francis taking too long? Or was he coming to the *wrong* conclusion so you hired me? I mean, hey, 25K is 25K—if Francis already accomplished his goal, I'm not going to throw a fit. It's not like we—"

Maxwell raised a hand to silence me. "Remember my phone call?"

"Yeah," I said, annoyed and confused.

"What's the last thing I asked you?"

Then I remembered.

He swallowed, made a funny face, and without looking at me (he was still looking out the window) he said, "I *had* thought that Francis took the retainer and fled. I think the young kids call it being 'ghosted.' He came into town. He sat where you're sitting now. I told him about Hector's neighbor, a man named Rowan Esko, and I believe he had the same contact as you regarding access to the lighthouse. Either way, he had access to the key. He used it."

"Who's Rowan Esko?" I said. "Why didn't you tell me—"

He raised a hand and I politely shut up.

"Rowan Esko died. And I thought that that literal dead end had been reason enough for Mr. Francis to take the money and abscond. Maybe he determined that without the testimony of Rowan Esko it was impossible to dig any deeper into Hector's innocence. Whatever the reason, I genuinely thought he'd quit—'ghosted' me—and *that's* why I never told you about it. About my hiring him. I didn't think it was relevant; and since he never left me any of his notes, it's not like I had anything to give you."

"Hold on," I said, thinking about his inquiring into my ownership of a firearm and being more than a little anxious about it. "Did Esko's death raise any red flags?"

"He had a myriad of health problems, both physical and psychological—PTSD, diabetic, legless, paranoid, and old—so I didn't bat an eye, nor did any of his surviving family, when I found out about his death. Nor did I overanalyze Mr. Francis's hasty up-and-leaving—I took it personally, of course, but I never sniffed any funkiness regarding . . . injurious outcomes. Or sinisterness.

"But"—he pressed a key and moved the mouse—"I have reason to believe, Mr. Trellis, that he did not *merely* up-and-leave, and that Rowan Esko did not *merely* die of natural causes. Or at least not completely natural causes. I'd like you to watch this."

He turned around the monitor and pressed ENTER on the keyboard.

I saw footage of a person—presumably John R. Francis—entering the lighthouse I was currently supposed to be investigating. He cut through the foyer; took a right and recorded—or rather (yes, Francis seemed like the pretentious type) *taped*—culty fish-nailed-to-crosses on the walls; and, when he got to the end of the hallway, he said, "*This is where, allegedly, the mother of the, um, young man . . . where she . . . well, where part of her was found.*" He continued to talk to Maxwell while filming. Then he bent down and rubbed the floor and said, "*Is that . . . ?*"

I glanced at Maxwell.

He nodded and said, "It is."

Dried blood.

The footage then showed Francis stand up and enter what was clearly the living quarters. A stairwell spiraled up, leading to the actual lighthouse portion of the timeworn building.

"This is where it happened," said Francis. *"Most of it, anyway. Except for the condemned's father, whose death and, um . . . post-mortem* bodily amendments *occurred up there in the lantern room. Which brings me to the reason for my being here, as well as this investigation. I think Truman Capote would have killed for this story."*

He walked deeper into the room.

A noise made gooseflesh crawl up my arm.

Francis stopped and spun in a circle and made a few cringeworthy statements on the architecture's beauty in contrast to the vileness of what had happened.

"Hold on," said Maxwell. Pressed a button. Pivoted the monitor back toward himself. "He's just going to talk about what the newspapers revealed about the killings, which you already know about. Let me get past this part." He used the mouse to change our point in the video timeline. "There," he said and turned the monitor back toward me and pressed ENTER.

"—found Hector Rowling in the middle of the room, covered in blood, a gore-covered ax in his hand—and he kept saying gibberish. Literal gibberish. Like another language—"

A click on the keyboard and the video paused.

"You didn't see it." More statement than question. "Watch the upper-righthand corner." He spun the monitor around, again fiddled with the timeline, turned it back toward me, and pressed ENTER again.

"—saying gibberish. Literal gibberish. Like another language—"

Now I saw it. Something flowy and black skittered behind the railings of the mezzanine overlooking the living quarters. "There's more. Look at the un-boarded-up window; it's clearly open, and . . ."

. . . and sure enough stood a figure in black, face obscured by a hood and something else, likely a mask, and a black van lingering behind it. The cloaked figure walked left. Francis hadn't seen it and kept talking to Maxwell—to *us*—across time and space.

"*You believe there might be something in Hector's bedroom that could prove his innocence. Perhaps a clue to who actually murdered his family. Not sure what that could be, Mr. Maxwell, but let's take a look. It's been six months, so I'm not so sure anything will be left—the police would've swept through everything. Not to mention the vandals, considering the graffiti.*"

Francis began walking up the steps. The stairwell hugged the wall until it led to the second-story mezzanine, which led to the lighthouse and also extended a little further, edging around the living room where there were three doors: one open, two closed.

"*The bedrooms,*" he said, peeking into the open doorway.

Revealed to me was a very small room. There were Harry Styles posters. An invasive specics of star-shaped stickers flamboyantly covered the walls. My Little Pony figurines guarded the pubescent expanse atop a dresser. "*This must be the sister's room. The police found her under the bed, against the wall.*" Francis made a sound I thought might've been gagging, but the decades'-old sound leaking from the speakers distorted it. "*She was able to tuck in her legs so Hector—sorry, the* killer—*couldn't reach her. The police know this because she had no scratches or bruises on her ankles or wrists, which would have indicated someone pulling her. No forensic clues to make it easier to either confirm Hector being the killer or to prove his innocence. The killer stood on the bed, used a hatchet like Jack Torrance, and cut through the frame.*" Francis grunted. "*Fucking monster.*"

An uncanny sense of *déjà vu* washed over me as I sat there swallowing with my eyes and ears the grainy footage and the mangled audio. I sat there dreamily watching Francis pull himself out of the sister's bedroom and make an exaggerated U-turn in the hall before arriving at the next door.

Francis tried the knob, which seemed to turn easily enough, and pushed it open. The door banged against the wall—its impact, contorted by the speakers, sounded like a harrowing scream. It was mostly dark in this room except for a flowy, ultra-black silhouette standing before the window, ringed by a halo of sunlight jittering like white worms sizzling on a hot skillet, as if the camera didn't know how to process the juxtaposition between sunlight, shade, and phantom; and a light cut through the room, showing an oddly angled bed, a stack of books on the floor, and the shadowy shape. It was *still* indecipherable. Even with the flashlight. And then Francis made a noise of emasculated startlement, whiny and frail—

As the camera fell to the floor, the flashlight beam washed over the figure in such a way that I imagined I saw something like a face, very pale and very long, with two black holes where eyes should be.

The shape moved forward, something in its hand.[6]

But Francis didn't turn off the camera.

It kept rolling.

Muttering of words. Not English. It sounded nasally and choppy, but somehow familiar.

Francis said only one word: "*Please.*"

---

[6] At the time I couldn't tell what it was, but I obviously know now—based on my own experiences—that it was a machete.

A *thwump!* sound. Silence. More muttered words and more silence and the camera jittered and shook violently as it rose into the air and slowly turned around, revealing a grainy, blackened face with huge eyes. It was too dark to make out details, the processing power of the camera at the limit of its low-light capabilities. The camera shook once more before it turned off.

For my sanity's sake, I could say only one thing:

"It could be fake." (And—sure—it *could* have been fake, it probably *should* have been fake, but it didn't *feel* fake.) "I mean . . . John R. Francis, from what I know about him, hangs around some Hollywood circles. Maybe he wanted the easy money and—you know—he made a fake video . . ."

I would have kept babbling had Maxwell (an undecipherable expression on his face) not bent down, reached into his drawer, and laid between us what looked like an archetypal handgun I'd seen in hundreds of movies and videogames, its form as pitch-dark as the grim fate it was fashioned to reap. The deadly thing pulled in my gaze like an evil magnet. Maxwell cleared his throat and I realized he'd placed a face-down Polaroid next to it.

"At first," he said, "I, too, thought it was fake. Then a few days ago I heard a knock at my door. I checked the surveillance feed, but couldn't quite make out the face. Something was *off.* He wore a long coat—"

"Like in the video?" I asked.

"Yes. But I hadn't seen the video yet, so I didn't make the connection. He drove off in a black van before I got the chance to stop him, or at least get his license plate number—although maybe that wasn't on my mind at the time. Might've been Jehovah's Witnesses for all I knew. Then I found this Polaroid on my front door mat. This *could* be fake, too, despite how real it looks, I understand, but, um, well, yes, here, look . . ." He let the sentence linger while flipping over the Polaroid and sliding it to me. It took maybe ten seconds before I knew what I was looking at, despite its *un*ambiguousness.

A puffed slit where the mutilated face's left eye should be while the right eye stared sleepily toward the picture-taker, an ugly miasma of unnatural colors orbiting either pupil; the nose removed; teeth too elongated, too straight, locked in a tortuous grin; long, wiry red- and blue-colored hair pressed in a painfully tight yet frizzy combover revealing a comically massive, almost rubber-looking forehead—plenty of space for the words INSIDE ESKO to arch over the thick, unvarying eyebrows; and there was nothing below the neck except for the stainless-steel table upon which it had been set. Scalpel at a diagonal. The composition made me think of an Instagram photo. And even if it was a real decapitated human head (John R. Francis's decapitated head) used as a sort of . . . *warning*, then why mutilate the face? It was so disfigured it could have been any Caucasian man's head.

I laughed.

Maxwell opened his mouth, confused.

"Now *that* looks fake—or at least *staged*."

Maxwell did a doubletake and said, "Fiddlesticks! You're sure? It really looks fake?"

"It does," I said.

He hummed and rubbed his chin and said, "Interesting. Well, regardless—that's still where I found the flash drive that contained Francis's footage."

"Where?" I said, but thought I knew.

"*Inside* Esko." He pointed to his Adam's apple. "Forced down his throat; postmortem."

"You had him reexamined?"

"Something like that." The man's eyes glinted in the

dim light. I could *feel* something like an omen in his words, in his eyes, which made me wonder if Maxwell had dug up the corpse himself. "I know what else you're going to say," he ventured, "that all of this could *still* be an elaborate hoax."

"Sure. The retainer fee alone might be worth it if Francis was in a tight spot for money."

"But two details poke holes in that. The first being, unlike with you and I, I hadn't written up a contract— he very well could have taken the money and left. He had no obligation other than, well . . . I guess something like journalistic *dignity*; if Francis had walked away, I would have frowned upon it, sure, but nothing more. Which brings me to the second detail: I found a severed finger just below the flash drive."

"Come again. Did you say—"

"A severed finger, yes, but I apologize for not having it on my person, otherwise I'd show you. I . . . I didn't know what to do with it, so I . . . got rid of it."

I hummed, not quite believing what I was hearing.

"It seems as though I'm being targeted," he said. "But by whom?"

He looked out the window, eyes jittering back and forth.

"It seems obvious to me . . ." said I, the skeptic of all things conspiratorial, stroppily convoluted, and everything else daring to rise above mundane or conventional wisdom (a disciple, you could say, of Occam's razor), and yet to assume John R. Francis was elaborately and macabrely pranking Maxwell was perhaps the most absurd of all logical pathways. ". . . that you need to call the police instead of hiring an investigative journalist such as myself," and I pushed away the black death-device.

Maxwell slammed his fist on the table, staring hot

little daggers into my eyes, causing me to almost fall out of my chair. His mouth opened and closed, twisted and constricted into a tight O. But all he said was, "I *can't.*" Then all tension released and he looked like a half-deflated, sad-looking balloon.

"I don't know who to trust. Not in this town. Not in any nearby town either. The police may even be *in* on it. *They* have a long reach, Felix, and I'm terribly tired."

"Then hire a fucking bodyguard. I am out of my element here, dude, with machete-maniacs and ax-murderers."

"Wasn't that always the risk, though?"

"*What?*"

"I mean," said Maxwell, "you took this job to investigate the possible *innocence* of Hector Rowling. If that happened to be the case—that he was innocent—obviously it would mean someone else—an ax-murderer, as you say—is still out there; that has always been the risk, wouldn't you agree?"

Instead of waiting for me to speak, he accurately translated the horror-infused incredulousness on my face and said, shrugging, "But sure. The part about their coming after me was unanticipated. Here, listen . . ." He pushed the gun back toward me, and I wanted to say I didn't even have a permit to carry one, let alone know how to use it, but I couldn't find my voice. "Just imagine"—and the officious little man actually put up his hands and spread them out—"headline news: Man sentenced to life in prison is found innocent. Or even *juicier*: Man sentenced to life in prison is found innocent and the killer is brought to justice. You'd be a celebrity, Mr. Trellis. You'd be able to get all of your pieces published in any major journal or magazine, get interviewed by Piers Morgan. The *prestige!* You might even sell a book or two. True crime sells, Felix, you know it does.

And, *hey hey hey—*"

He opened a drawer, bent down, and rummaged for something before slapping down the *something* on the table—a bunch of greenish rectangles made of cotton and linen fibers. Dozens upon dozens of Benjamin Franklins looked up at me. Maxwell pushed the dead presidents toward me.

"It's yours. Take it and leave, or take it and stay. *It's yours it's yours it's yours.*"

It was a bit too much cash money to ignore, and before my brain knew what my hands were doing they were scooping up and neatly stacking the hundred-dollar bills into a pile. It ended up being a modest brick. Five thousand dollars.

"And here," said Maxwell, holding out a hot pink My Little Pony flash drive (at that moment I assumed it had belonged to his daughter). "The killer was also kind enough to include an audio recording of Francis's conversation with Esko—"

"How'd the killer get access to that?" I was once again thinking of a grand and elaborate hoax.

And once again he used his weaselly, quasi-freaky insight and said, "I know, I know. It's fishy—the killer finding where John had been staying and getting onto his laptop. But consider this: maybe they only injured him in the video—then forced the information from him. Before killing him. Or . . . *whatever.*

"Either way," Maxwell continued, making a sound more whale song than sigh. "We can only postulate— and wouldn't you agree that that gets us nowhere? Even if Francis wanted half the money—and decided to make an elaborately produced indie film and fabricated masked, cloaked figures to deflect any discredit that could be said of his work ethic—there's still the matter of Hector's innocence. Heck, if you want to disregard any of the masked-killer stuff and just focus on the material facts—what little there are, alas—then I don't blame you, Felix."

"I'll see where this rabbit hole takes me," I said with finality. I reached over for the black death-device, at first not knowing what to do with it, then gingerly ("the safety's on," he told me, accurately deciphering my hesitancy) slid it under my jeans' waistband for no other reason than that was how I'd seen Hollywood solve the actor-without-a-holster problem. I didn't like the feeling of it against my skin. Then I grabbed the hot pink flash drive, tucked it into my pocket.

Ron Ullman commences his vividly imaginative depiction of the inception of the Festival of the Fish (and consequently the Church of the Fish) with an approach befitting that of a horror film. The atmosphere is set with an eerie stillness of the wind and the sky, which is described as being "ablaze with unprecedented hues" (which, I feel compelled to say, is almost word-for-word copied from the recovered journal of Charlie Blackwood). Ullman, conveniently in order to fill in the gaps, makes bountiful leaps of creative liberty due to severe flooding (some indiscernible time earlier) in the archives having rendered portions of the journal illegible, among one other factor that Ullman addresses in Chapter 3; what we can, however, make out is this:

> *[The water] was fraught with a sense of foreboding expectancy, and I swear to you that fins of creatures that were not quite sharks, but almost sharks, were circling in that eerily dark expanse. Those who encircled me—my family, some acquaintances, my*

spouse—were seized by a frenzy of apocalyptic proportions. My cousin Tracy swooned, hit her head on a rock, then proceeded to prattle on about the "beast from the sea." At that time, having only touched the Holy Bible to use it as a doorstopper, I had not known to what she was referencing. Yet her words appeared to spread like a contagion, and Tracy's husband, Tomas, became wide-eyed, uttering from Revelation Thirteen *like a mantra. He dashed around the encampment shouting it out, and sometimes he added "chapter thirteen verses one through ten" to the mantra. Some of us appeared to comprehend what he was saying, eyes widening in terror and adding to the mass delirium. Yet others, including myself and the children, were only frightened and moderately perplexed; I myself did not quite understand what I'd seen, only that it filled me with* A SENSE OF AWE; *my wife raised her hands in the air and spoke in an unknown tongue, causing someone to label her a "WITCH!" and leading me to strike that person in the face. (I have lately built a new barn on his property as a feeble form of reparation.) I then thought that God had swiftly converted my wife to His will, and that she was praying to Him. ~~I know now that that wasn't quite the case~~.*[7]

---

[7] In the present discourse, Ullman indulges in a chapter-long exegesis concerning the implications of Blackwood's written work and the reasons behind his subsequent scribbling out of the same. Drawing from his extensive body of research and scholarship on the matter, he postulates that the Church of the Fish, which figures prominently in Blackwood's text, may have been affiliated with a

. . . I looked out into the darkly foaming ocean, teeming with GREAT LIFE; *and Tomas—now among many others—continued to recite from the End Times, chanting thus—*

". . . the sand of the sea, and saw a beast rise up out of the sea, having seven heads and ten horns, and upon his horns ten crowns, and upon his heads

---

cult dedicated to the veneration of Dagon. It is worth noting, however, that Howard Phillips Lovecraft (the celebrated American writer of horror and weird fiction) did not publish his seminal short story "Dagon" until the year 1919, a full five years subsequent to Ullman's interview with Dr. Wallace Redman (an academic living in ███████), and the only record of Ullman mentioning the Dagon-connection. Thus, the precise reason for both Ullman and Lovecraft's attribution of a nautical connotation to Dagon—a deity conventionally associated with the domains of agriculture, fertility, and grain—remains unclear and may well be a mere coincidence.

Readers seeking to further acquaint themselves with the multifarious strands of lore and myth surrounding the themes of the sea and its mysteries are advised to peruse the erudite work *Sealore and Stranger Things* by Dr. Wallace Redman, posthumously published by Oakhouse Publishing in 1966.

the name of blasphemy. And the beast which I saw was like unto a leopard, and his feet were as the feet of a bear, and his mouth as the mouth of a lion: and the dragon . . ."[8]

Verily, naught occurred after the spectacle of what I now believe was the LITERAL HAND OF GOD—albeit some opine that it was one of the Lord's archangels come to deliver us; why dispute semantics when the outcome is the same?—and HIS squeezing the life out of that GREAT FISH.

Tomas stood in the sea, its saltiness up to his knees, his image betwixt neurotic and valiant, and continued he did burbling about four angels standing in the four corners of the earth to prevent any wind from blowing on the land. Perchance he recited from memory the entire book of Revelation, but I presently dozed off, the awe having drained every ounce of power within me, and perhaps also the paradoxically redundant and circular sensation of feeling scared that I was not scared. As I pen this, I reckon it may be due to Alma's peculiar steadfastness and all that night her muttering over and over "We are chosen we are chosen we are chosen"; her nonsensical chatter, in any other circumstance, would have bothered me enough to abscond to the other side of the encampment; but this was not [any other circumstance] and her crooning soothed me as I lay my head on her legs.

Looking up to the heavens.

Specks of white against the deepest of blacks, a thin veneer over a deeper truth.

Dreams of leviathans and nameless creatures whose structures my dreaming mind couldn't quite

---

[8] *Revelation* 13 : 1-2

grasp.

Then a scream, and the Manna, *and our salvation (or—as Alma put it—our "Chosenness"), and my being called out of that* ABYSS *to fish for others stuck in that very same sewage of worry and aimlessness and aloneness and fear, and the Church and its calling.*

At this point, Ullman claims the remainder of Blackwood's journal is illegible—not because of water damage, let alone any other form of environmental wear and tear, but because of spilled ink. This is where we have to negotiate realms of the absurd and venturous suppositions as we trust in the validity of Ullman's "scientific" findings with nothing in our disadvantageous placement on the timeline to permit us to falsify or verify his claims. Ullman allegedly sent the ink-stained journal to a Harvard University lab run by a Dr. Ichabod Glenworshin, who seemed not only to be a correspondent with Ullman but a close friend as well—likely due to their shared appetite for the esoteric.

"Dr. Glenworshin doesn't restore the document in its entirety," Ullman writes in *A Dark History of the Families of the Fish.* "But he does find the following key words and phrases in the blotted mess, in chronological order:

". . . Midnight Coach . . . Dag Elohim . . . must [construct] the Lighthouse **:** **//==----{data can't be read}----**

ANSWER THE CALL

----{**data recovered**}----==\\ : t e Dar   us

". . . owling [possibly 'howling'; 'growling'; or the surname of Blackwood's wife's maiden name, 'Rowling'] . . . [s]acrificium sanguini[s][9] . . . unsheathed hand of YHWH, I hear IT tapping under the waves on the sea bottom; it's calling us [home]."

Ullman furthermore believes that the ink stain was not by accident; that either Charlie Blackwood, his wife Alma, or another person—maybe a descendent—found his confessions too implicating for the community; that perhaps spilled ink was the preferred method of expunging the passages, favoring its low-key resemblance to mishap, over something as obtuse and obvious as ripping out the page.

Which brings me to, perhaps, the most frustrating aspect of Ullman's literary work. It's his relentlessness not just beating but absolutely *decimating* the vicinity around the black bush of this town's history. He all but says he believes, as if saying it out loud would put his life in danger, that the origins of the Festival of the Fish (as well as the juxtapositive Church) is steeped in something covertly occult. To moreover muddy the already too-tortuous waters, in the year 1981 the local police found Ullman murdered at the ripe age of 81, in Charlotte, MI, where he'd retired with his wife (also murdered) and ten-year-old grandson, Ron Ullman Jr., the third of his name.

Ron Ullman Jr.—whose internet persona is *Wayward Ron*—survived what the papers called *The Charlotte Farmhouse Massacre*. Since then, he has expanded his grandfather's conspirative legacy and currently has five "historical" novels published by Axiom (their factuality must be considered with a huge, raised eyebrow).

---

[9] Latin translation for "Blood Sacrifice."

THE WORDS *"CALL ME ISHMAEL"* tumbled across my mind as I braved against the unadulterated unknown-ness of the lighthouse on the hill, overlooking ███████████ like an odd pagan idol. However, up close it appeared even more off-putting than a mere "idol"; the word with which to replace it lost somewhere deep in my psycho-sphere, rattling around in a mental crevice, irritating my thoughts—yet not quite graspable.

Call me Ishmael.

I looked under the pink rock that lay in a forgotten, weed-choked garden off to the side of the lighthouse. I had half expected it to be gone (and wholly hoped it would be), but there it lay in a bed of mulch, and there my hand reached for the skeleton key; it was easier to grasp than the allusive word adversely superseding "idol."

Call me Ishmael.

Thunder overhead, rumbling in impenetrably dense, far away cumuli; a phantasmic mountain range deep in the sea . . .

(. . . and thinking about those clouds now, I seri-ously wonder if perhaps they weren't "clouds," strictly speaking, but a home—an astral plane—for the "GREAT DOVE," i.e., "GOD'S HAND." Madness, I know, but considering what I've since seen . . .)

. . . it was 6 PM.

They come like clockwork after 7, the woman from *The Fish Tavern* had texted me. At the time I thought she meant a caretaker or a routine drive-through by the local police, but when I felt the heaviness of the skeleton key in my hand—the temporal trepidation surging through my fingers, one brought on by what felt like

(*Ishmael*)

the inversion of déjà vu: I hadn't done this before, hadn't been here before, shouldn't have been here at all; it was some strange glitch the GREAT CODER hadn't expected me to find, had specifically designed *existentia* and all its many dark or weird or mundane tributaries for me and my limited beingness and others of my meat-suit-restricted variety to, in fact, *not* find—I was no longer certain by what she'd meant by "they."

Far from the pretentious, pinky-raised-while-drinking-tea-and-jacking-off-to-*Citizen Kane* douchebagery of John R. Francis, I did not use an unnecessarily obsolete 90s videotape camera to record my passage into the lighthouse; after I slid the key into the lock and opened the moaning door, I pulled out my phone and used it primarily for a flashlight, secondarily as a camera. In my other hand I held the gun. The safety was on. I didn't want to shoot a teenager with a spray-paint can, a caretaker, or (Lord forbid) a cop, by mistake; no, I had the gun more for purposes of intimidation. And because I still didn't quite believe Francis wasn't pranking the conspiratorial-minded Maxwell.

I walked into the lighthouse's living quarters.

NOTHING BUT EARTH TONES IN the modest mudroom and vestibule.

Nothing but a bench in the mudroom and a table in the vestibule.

Nothing on or under the bench, nothing on or under the table—except for a small half-circle imprint in the liberal layers of dust, and even the imprint itself had begun to grow a film of dust.

John C. Francis hadn't checked the room to the left; therefore, to be thorough, I did—and immediately regretted it. It was a foul-smelling room (I still smell like a sunbaked, dead sea-thing as I write this).

There was an oak desk. Terribly worn out. Gouges decorating it like a bullet-riddled war relic. Someone had placed a dead crab—its legs impossibly long, almost arachnid—on top of the desk; had spread it out occultly, its legs neatly and evenly stretched out so as to make it look like a rudimentary star; and then had meticulously splayed it open so its crabby innards pooled in an area before it. Some unknown finger had etched what looked like a fish into its mushy guts as if it were a primitive iconographic expression in an upside-down thought bubble.

I awkwardly set down the gun and pulled my shirt above my nose and mouth and pulled open the drawers in the desk, but I found nothing except an apocryphal copy of *The Second Book of Jonah.*

I flipped through it for a clue, but only found hazy sermons.

6:05 PM.

I moved on. Through the vestibule, through the

(*DAG ELOHIM*)

(*Ishmael*)

hallway, where at the end the police had found the decapitated head of Rita Rowling (also, like the crab, *occultly displayed*). She was the daughter of a fisherman named Frank Ullman, who'd died of cancer in '12, and his wife Margot, who's still living today and who sells her nautical-themed watercolor paintings during the Festival (it's rumored that her paintings have gotten much darker since the murder of her daughter and her daughter's family). And, as with the crab, Jonah's fish had ornamented the ground below her head. I stopped here to soak in the ghostly memory with my light, and I knelt down and found myself reaching my hand toward it. The dark stain remained, as did portions of the chalk in which the fish and cock had been drawn. Then I touched it.

I MUST PAUSE HERE BECAUSE it's fundamental for everything that follows. You could say this is a "nexus event," even if at the time it had been nearly and immediately forgotten after it had occurred. Before touching the blood stain I think I started feeling lightheaded, but thought nothing of it. I may even have seen some stars sizzle across my vision, but there were no *nightfish* yet.

But anyway.

Like I said: I touched the bloodstain.

Then something happened.

I hallucinated, slipped through some fissure in reality, tripped balls, dreamt the dream of the lighthouse, the dream of ███████████, of the Fish—but I didn't actually remember it until the dream/vision recurred later on; and each time since, I've remembered more and more.

I dreamt I had never fallen into that dream; dreamt I'd won a Pulitzer for some obscure work I'd written; dreamt I met a fabricated woman named Samina (in the dream she didn't have a face, it was indistinct and murky, but I sensed she was beautiful); dreamt we had children and they grew up and had children of their own and their children had children and their children had children, but I was still alive, watching my many descendants scuttle across the ocean floor on their stilted legs. Black, shadowy fish swam around them, zigzagging ravenously about the Great Brood, eating my children and their children and their children—but I didn't seem to care. Nor did they. I walked beyond my colony, the mudflat swirling with sediment as I lifted and extended one foot at a time, onward, the sea darker but somehow still visible. The Great Brood were crying for me to come back as the big black fish continued to reduce their numbers. But I kept going.

Eventually I found a deep chasm.

I looked down into it.

I saw a hand.

I saw a dove.

I saw a daemon.

Whatever I saw was hazy: a black silhouette against an even blacker black. It moved, that shape, and that's when I found—to my left, at the lip of the abyss—the Abyss—no, the ABYSS—the very rough first draft of the manuscript for my Pulitzer prize-winning work (the *dream-me* always wrote in longhand, even though I was aware—vaguely, anyway—that the *real-me* used Microsoft Word).

THE SWALLOWED TOWN was writ in

(*blood*)

red, and I began to read from it.

HOST

Well . . . since we're going *THERE*, Mr. Ullman, I gotta ask about the goddamn elephant in the room. I've listened to you on other podcasts, you know, and you seem to brush the topic away. But despite having five novels in the New York Times bestseller list, you never voyage *THERE*. And I always find that odd because of the

[*stutters*]

bizarre places you navigate in some of the United States' darkest histories. You know what I'm going to ask, don't you?

"WAYWARD" RON ULLMAN JR.

I've got my suspicions, but I'd rather have you define the "elephant in the room" so as to avoid my going off on a radically different train of thought.

HOST

[*laughter*]

Fair enough. Okay, so you were *there* that night.

"WAYWARD" RON ULLMAN JR.

You're talking 1965?

HOST

Absofuckinlutely. You're, what, thirteen?

"WAYWARD" RON ULLMAN JR.

[*a beat*]

Ten.

HOST

Ten years old.

[*whistles*]

And your grandfather is quite elderly at this point, right? In his eighties, I would guess.

"WAYWARD" RON ULLMAN JR.

Yessir. Depends on one's definition of elderly, but yes, eighty—

[*calculates*]

—two, eighty-three. Something like that.

HOST

And why?

"WAYWARD" RON ULLMAN JR.

Why what?

HOST

I mean, on top of you never talking about *that* night, you've never . . . from what I understand, and I might be wrong . . . you've never talked about what happened to your parents, which was, I assume, the catalyst for living with your grandparents.

"WAYWARD" RON ULLMAN JR.

They died when I was eight.

HOST

Fuck.

[*a beat*]

Is this off-limits?

"WAYWARD" RON ULLMAN JR.

[*sighs*]

I suppose not.

HOST

Okay, well, we certainly have a can of worms to open. I guess—yeah—okay—we start chronologically—and if this is in any way uncomfortable, just say "Fuck you, Georgie," and we'll move on. Sounds good?

"WAYWARD" RON ULLMAN JR.

Fine as wine, Georgie.

HOST

How did your parents die?

"WAYWARD" RON ULLMAN JR.

[*ruffling fabric*]

You want me to say they were brutally murdered or died under *mysterious* circumstances. Sorry to disappoint you, but it was apparently just plain old Leptospirosis.

HOST

[*to assistant*]

Can you look that up, Scott? Starts with an L, not a G—where'd you come up with a fuckin' G? Yeah; l, e, p, t, o, s—yeah, there . . .

[*mumbling*]

. . . bacterial infection . . . contact with water contaminated by the urine . . . marine mammals . . . swimming, diving, or working in waterlogged environments . . . a wide range of symptoms, from mild flu-like sickness to severe complications affecting multiple organs.

[a beat]

Okay, well, I'm sorry for your loss. That must have been hard on a kid.

"WAYWARD" RON ULLMAN JR.

[*uncanny laughter*]

I don't remember much.

HOST

At the time of their deaths, were you living in ██████████?

"WAYWARD" RON ULLMAN JR.

Around the time of my father's sixteenth birthday or so, my grandparents relocated to Florida. My grandfather's first draft of *A Dark History of the Fish* in ████████ —or *of the Families of the Fish,* to be more precise. Never understood why he named it such a long title. I guess it makes it sound more important, which I think it is . . . to a niche group. So, no. My father met my mother at the University of Michigan; both were students there. My grandparents would visit him on occasion, which was how they got familiar enough with Michigan to move out there after my parents died.

HOST

Ah. So your parents maybe moved back to

[*a beat*]

Florida after they graduated from U of M, which explains the marine

[*another beat*]

-oriented disease.

"WAYWARD" RON ULLMAN JR.

No. We were living on the outskirts of Ann Arbor, Michigan, at the time. My mother was closer to her family than my dad was to his—I think it had to do with my grandfather's obsession with ████████ rubbed my dad the wrong way. It wasn't healthy being around. Mentally, that is.

[*a beat*]

I hear the gears in your conspiratorial brain turning, Georgie. It's not impossible to catch

Leptospirosis in Michigan.

HOST

But probably unlikely.

"WAYWARD" RON ULLMAN JR.

[*likely a shrug*]

HOST

You would think your grandparents *wouldn't* want to live in the same state their *only son* and daughter-in-law passed away in. I'm assuming they made the move specifically for you, correct?

"WAYWARD" RON ULLMAN JR.

I was only eight at the time. To be honest, I didn't have any friends. And my grandparents didn't even move to Ann Arbor. No. No, I think something spooked my grandfather; I think even Florida—and mind you, living as far inland in Florida as possible—was a little too close to

[*a beat*]

the coast. The ocean terrified him. But I think writing about it—███████—felt like a calling. Like . . . he felt he had a responsibility.

HOST

Ah, ladies and gentlemen, we've come full circle to the morbidly obese elephant in the room. Let's hear it, Ron. What's the connection?

"WAYWARD" RON ULLMAN JR.

Well. Before we get into *that*, it's crucial for me to correct you on something you said a minute earlier. It's one of the ways my grandfather was continuously getting info on the F███████ and the Ch████. My father wasn't their only son.

HOST

Ohhhhh.

"WAYWARD" RON ULLMAN JR.

My uncle was about ten years older than my father. He'd already established himself in ████████████. He stayed behind—but I can't really say much more than that, just in case . . .

HOST

[*laughs*]

In case of *what*? Ronnie, you're in your fifties—

"WAYWARD" RON ULLMAN JR.

—I'm almost sixty—

HOST

—if your uncle—*sixty*? You look great for your age, man. As I was saying, if your uncle is still alive—

"WAYWARD" RON ULLMAN JR.

—oh, he isn't—

HOST

—then what's the deal? Who are you protecting?

"WAYWARD" RON ULLMAN JR.

My uncle has children so I can't get into any more details—for their safety.

HOST

[*whispers*]
Can you tell me off-air?

"WAYWARD" RON ULLMAN JR.

[*indecipherable muttering*]

HOST

Well, Ronnie, I gotta tell ya, man, we're veering off course here. We need to delve into what the hell went down on that night back in 1965.

"WAYWARD" RON ULLMAN JR.

Okay, *well.*

[*sighs*]

I remember it like it was yesterday. I still feel the, um, icy floor. That was immediately odd because my grandmother ran cold, so my saintly grandfather would always crank up the heat for her. But yes, I remember the cold floor. I didn't look at the clock but I thought it was around nine or so. It was October so it got dark relatively early—although, I discovered from the cops weeks later that it was just past 3 AM. I lived upstairs and heat rises, you know, and even though I usually opened the window— even in winter—I was surprised by how damn cold it was. It's kind of like having an uncanny dream that you're sitting in your living room and

[*a beat*]

something just feels *off.* You can't explain it. There's no monster. *Yet.* The uncanniness feels like evidence of there being—you know—an *off-screen wrongness*; and that very abstract forbiddingness is what actually *lures* the monster. So yes, the cold floor, and I thought maybe I was having the opposite of a waking nightmare—maybe I was awake but thought I was dreaming . . . at any rate, I got up and put on my socks and I

[*stutters*]

dreamwalked to the window that looked over the front yard, and I saw what at first thought was—in fact, what my pre-adolescent brain deciphered as—a big black shark or . . . *something*. Lying still. Very, *very* still. On my driveway. Big dull eyes staring at me. Challenging me. Then it swam away, wraithlike, down our long and windy driveway, through the trees, to the road, and it vanished. I don't remember what happened next. But apparently I kept telling the 911 dispatcher "*the shark took their heads the shark took their heads the shark took their heads.*" The dispatcher also claimed I said "*the shark put* 'a dog below him.'"

IN THE WANING DAYS OF autumn, when the ██████ shivers beneath a pallid sky, I found myself upon the desolate coast of ████████████████████████, where ████████ lurk and ██████ are obscured. Here, amidst the blackly foaming tides crashing upon the shore, an enigmatic ██████████ graces the land. They call it *Matanah Ne'evah,* a glorious gift brought forth by the relentless ocean currents.

Year after year, the *Matanah Ne'evah* emerge from the depths, their arrival shrouded in ██████. Only during the witching hours of the night, between the specter of 3 AM and the twilight's lingering breath at 5 AM, does it manifest itself. This

mihole gad eht fo maerd maerd a maerd a ylno maerd a ylno si siht maerd a ylno si

offering remains for a fleeting duration, sometimes a day, sometimes two. Yet the longest recorded occurrence, an anomaly witnessed by ████████████████ ████████ in the annals of 1817, extended its divine reign for a baffling span of ten days.

These fragments of knowledge, haphazardly gathered, were bestowed upon me through an inconspicuous ██████████, stumbled upon during my matutinal trek on the second day of my arrival at this weather-beaten town on the outskirts of ~~Carcosa~~. It bore a weighty invitation, urging me to uncover the veiled truths at the Academy of the Dag—a society marinated in the laborious toil of native █████████, zealous █████████, and other fervent █████████. Together, they strive to preserve the cryptic origins of the *Matanah Ne'evah*, laboring to disentangle the gnarled web of mythology and salvage morsels of veracity, or at least a semblance thereof.

Yet I must confess

that i did not stop them from carrying out their ritual   it was a necessary correction you see   a misalignment caused by uncle bill running from responsibility   running from DAG ELOHIM

but you did not kill your family   physically i mean   that is what im asking

i let them in   i let them ~~behead my mother~~   *i watched when they   did that   to* ~~my sister~~ *and* ~~my father~~   *oh blessed be* DAG ELOHIM

that my presence in this strange vicinity was not tethered to the siren call of their festival, which these strange dream-denizens call The Solemnity of Dag Elohim. Hidden motives propelled my journey, motivations divergent from the quaint curiosities and sun-bleached charm that this hamlet exuded.

But before visiting the Academy of the Dag—in fact, this happened the night before at the local watering hole called The Dagwood—a woman had approached me: she of almost-black hair, almost-black eyes, and almost-black clothes—the attire of an attendant at a classy funeral; her skin fair as paper, smooth, ageless . . . *timeless.*

I nodded to her as I rested on my elbow against the bar top. In my other hand a Bloody Mary wobbled. And she smiled and said matter-of-factly, "You're not from around here."

"Guilty. What gave me away?"

"Your suit and tie. Alma." She proffered her too-white hand.

It should have been cold. But it was hot, as if she'd had her hand too close to a fire. I smelled woodsmoke.

I sipped my Bloody Mary. No—I gulped it, and it tasted like seawater.

"Do you know that God has plans for you?"

I choked. Couldn't help but stifle a laugh.

"Whoa, lady, we just met."

"Your point being?" A smile curled her mouth. She laughed. "I'm just fucking with you. Sorry, not very lady-like—that language. I thought maybe you were a Jehovah's Witness, what with the way you dressed, so I was testing the waters."

I looked down, embarrassed. She had a point.

What brings you to ███████████?

"Excuse me?" I said.

"I didn't say anything." Then she ordered "what he's having," and the bartender looked at *what he's having,* nodded, vanished. She turned back to me. "But I was going to ask: what brings you to ██████████?"

"Job."

"No shit." She exaggeratedly eyed my suit and tie. "What job?"

"Well, a man has hired me to do research and write an article on a man who's in prison for a most . . . abysmal thing. My employer believes this man is innocent."

"I hear about that happening often: public interest in a case becoming a catalyst for the justice system to virtue signal their way into double-checking their evidence. That's what your article is meant to do?"

"That's the plan," I said and took another drink.

"Did you visit him?" she asked. "Hecky, I mean."

"Hecky? Oh, yeah, Hector Rowling. Yes, but he's absolutely insane."

"So he *did* do the 'abysmal thing?'" She raised an eyebrow.

I shrugged and gulped my poison and sighed and turned to face her and took another drink before setting down my glass. I then gave her my fullest, rawest, most endearing focus.

"Not necessarily. I can't be certain, but it seems as though what I perceive as 'insane' may just be a symptom of something else. PTSD. I've done some research on it. It happens."

"I heard he confessed." The bartender gave her her drink and she smiled at him and the bartender avoided her eyes—in fact, he seemed frightened by her. I hardly noticed it at the time; I'd assumed it was her other-worldly beauty that intimidated him. But thinking back on it now, writing this as my fourth whisky sits beside me like a psychic-protective totem, I *do* think it was a genuine boogeyman type of fear. Of course it was. And I now almost know why.

Anyway.

I told her: "Police often abuse verbal confession as the all-defining smoking gun, but there are plenty of times when people confess to crimes in which they did not partake, either in order to get it over with (the interrogation, I mean), or sometimes the police sort of *brainwash them* into thinking they actually did it. A lot of times low-IQ people confess to crimes they did not commit. How well did you know Hector?"

"Well enough to call him Hecky."

"I've heard he was a normal boy—before what had happened. Is that true?"

"Depends on what 'normal' means. He was devout to the Church, which to an outsider—an irreligious person—could be perceived as 'abnormal.'"

She had another point.

So I then specified: "Was he—I guess there's no other way of saying it—was he . . . *slow*?"

She paused and seemed to think on it. "I, of course, am not privy as to his school grades. He was always a quiet boy. Very obedient to the ███."

I felt a chill. "What do you mean by that?"

"Here." From her purse—of course it was almost-black—she pulled out a piece of paper and, using a pen (almost-black), scribbled down something. Before showing me she asked, "Have you been there?"

"Where?"

"You know where."

Did I?

She clarified: "The crime scene."

"No. My employer is passionate, yes, but is a social outcast. He's got money but has no ins. So to speak. That's why he hired me. Unless you have a key." I laughed so as to show her my jest.

She slid over the note.

324

"What's this?"

"You'll know." She picked up the pen again. "What's your number?"

Hesitantly I told her.

"I'm on the city council. Unlike your employer, I *do*

have some ins. I'll leave you a copy of the key to the
Darkhouse. And I'll text you where to find it. I'll
remind you tomorrow, but you should be gone by seven
PM."

"Why?"

"Because I don't want you to ███████████. And also
DAG ELOHIM has plans for you."

Before I could ask "what the fuck does that mean?"
she was gone.

THE STRANGELY TITLED MANUSCRIPT—not necessarily metaphysical, but rather . . . *psychophysical*—went on in a reality adjacent to my own in an almost purple prose, sometimes so gratingly reliant on my *dream-self* having been consciously aware of my *real-self*'s original journal (which, unlike my *dream-self* who seemed to be writing a quasi-fictional novelette or a novella, the *real-me* was only chronicling the events in ████████, so as to effectively write the article per Maxwell's hiring of me, and to possibly, if truly innocent, exonerate Hector Rowling) . . . and yet other times the manuscript was so paradoxically and starkly *un*connected: such as on page 41, when I—*dream-I*—had written about an extracosmic beach, stars misaligned overhead and too big, and on this beach a primordial shark (or whale) lay, and perched atop it stood a great and terrible bird (the progenitor of all eagles, maybe), its talons digging in and out of its fishy prey for eternity in an entangled predator-prey conciliation; and a black ooze—a black *living* ooze—trickled out of the shark whale whatever, squiggling squirming singing begging sobbing for someone anyone anything to just keep it company; and something about the sand—*dream-I* wrote—was too white to be earth-sand; then *dream-I* started writing about how he I we

were in a motel somewhere, but a man—Nakey Jakey, he called himself—warned the Protagonist to leave, warned him that another resident writer—*THE WANDER- ING PROPHET OF THE LUNARIS DEVERSORIUM*—would be seeking him and that he, the Protagonist (which I think is *me*), should run, so he I we did. Then suddenly the writer of *The Swallowed Town*, on page 51, seemed to pretend none of the stuff on the beach or the abrupt transferal to a desolate motel in the middle of nowhere, one with no cars and a red moon looming overhead, had even happened—or if it had happened, then it had no significance, and there was no other mention of THE WANDERING PROPHET—for in the very next paragraph there was a swift and dizzyingly disjointed continuation of his my our investigation of the ~~light~~house : //==----
{data can't be read}

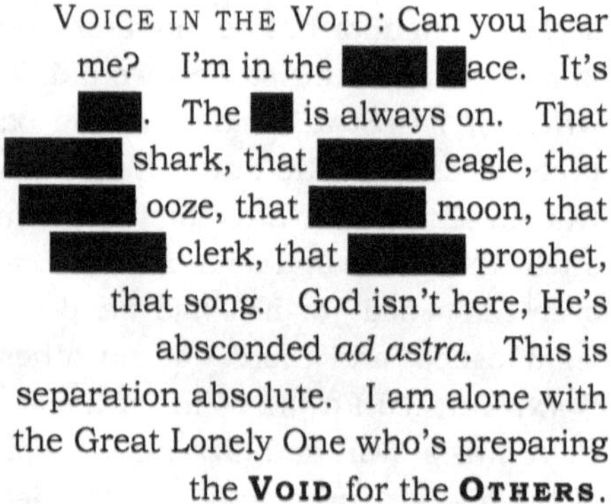

VOICE IN THE VOID: Can you hear me?   I'm in the ███ █ace.   It's ███.   The █ is always on.   That █████ shark, that ██████ eagle, that █████ ooze, that ██████ moon, that █████ clerk, that █████ prophet, that song.   God isn't here, He's absconded *ad astra*.   This is separation absolute.   I am alone with the Great Lonely One who's preparing the **VOID** for the **OTHERS**.

Their zealous and ravenous quest to **TSALAL** resulted in their most dreadful, most macabre plummet into the degenerative maw of **NIGHT**.

I am ████.   Can you hear me?   324 opens the door.   ████ find me.   There's █ hope left.

{**data recovered**}----==\\ : darkhouse. Also, retreading my own chronicled events in *slanted* ways (e.g., "the Solemnity of Dag Elohim" instead of "the Festival of the Fish," "Matanah Ne'evah" instead of "Sea Manna") didn't seem to deter me or cause alarm to my seemingly oblivious *dream-self.* Perhaps I remember feeling a sense of déjà vu—and yet I only speculate; while I remember the details of the dream—in fact, very specific details— obscure aspects, like the names of my children and, in savant mode, word for word the entire manuscript of *The Swallowed Town*—I don't remember specific *feelings.* In my dream (if you can call it that; perhaps "hallucination" is a better word) I also didn't seem impressed by my being able to read from a manuscript not only in the sea but at the very bottom of it. In darkness absolute.

That's when I heard it—whatever *it* was, from its depths—thus jolting my dream-eyes from *The Swallowed Town* manuscript; and when I looked down again to see if the noise-making shape had emerged from the endless chasm and into this lesser aquatic darkness—to see what owned such a mutilated, haunted whale song— I lost my footing and I fell. I floated. Unable to swim. My children's children's children

(*chanting*)

crying behind me at the chasm's edge, their clatter- ing, chattering claws like death-metal drums; *clop clop clop clop clop* sang their melancholic medley; and the deeper I fell, the louder their song.

And again—a deep vibration, almost but *not quite* coming from the colossal hand-shaped leviathan at the bottom. Again the *brhhhhhhh brhhhhhh brhhhhhhh.* And a light: another sun: blinding: "what the

(*lighthouse the lighthouse the lighthouse the*)

fuck?" I said, choking on what tasted too metallic to be saliva, the dream of the ABYSS and the reading of *The*

Swallowed Town manuscript at its

   (*maw*)

   edge for now a forgotten dream.

The leviathan was hand-shaped because it was a hand—*my* hand; at that bottomless chasm, beyond a black veil of an even blacker dream, my hand was touching the bloodstain from Rita Rowling's severed head. And that's when I

   (*he*)

   (*it*)

   (*the hand*)

suddenly stood, only vaguely aware of having what you might call a sort of "psychedelic trip," my heart thrusting into my throat. I brought the buzzing phone to my ear, which extinguished all light except for what bent around the corner from the vestibule and the light behind me, cutting through the boarded-up windows in the next room.

Unknown number.

"Hello?" I said disorientedly.

No answer.

Voices though. Indistinct. Like someone having butt-dialed me at a party. I can't remember if I hung up or if the caller did—I only recall turning on my phone's flashlight and flicking its glow into what I'd normally call a Living Room, now a Dead Room: a disorienting miasma of charnel-hued shadows; vortexes of slow-churning dust motes, stagnantly indifferent to my presence; spiderwebs spread across the ceiling-corners, the sheet-covered furniture, and the curtains, whose eight-legged corpses bled through shallow graves of pale dirt; and ontological memories I felt I could almost reach.

It felt like déjà vu.

Well, no, not quite.

Because I *had* already trodden this place, time and

time again. Just not physically. You see, when I'd gotten back to the inn after meeting with Maxwell, I immediately plugged the My Little Pony flash drive into my MacBook. I'd read some of Francis's notes—the ones the killer had so politely extracted from his laptop—and I'd listened to the recorded conversation between John R. Francis and eccentrically scatterbrained Rowan Esko. But it was the lighthouse footage that fascinated me most. I watched it five or six times before driving to the lighthouse myself. Maybe I saw it as a kind of cheat sheet, as if by memorizing the moments before John's (alleged) death, I could somehow spare myself the same fate. (I'm writing this now, so perhaps it worked in some roundabout, unknowable way . . . although I fear I only prolonged the inevitable.)

Gooseflesh skittered up my arms and legs when I first looked up into the mezzanine, half expecting to find a cloaked figure standing in the corner. I thought of its mask. Or—God forbid—its actual face. I thought of the dog, during the *annum* of 1650, with its eyes hollowed out, roses jammed into its sockets. Then I looked to the window. Even if a cloaked figure had stood there, with a black van idling through the window behind it, I wouldn't have been able to see it—someone had boarded up the window since Francis's venture here.

I checked my phone.

6:11 PM.

Plenty of time.

Something I realized upon my third revisitation of the Francis footage was the time in the lower right-hand corner: 7:23. He must not have received the same warning as I had; and did that doom him, and did that save me? Who's to know for certain, except that, yes—

They come like clockwork after 7,

the woman from the bar had texted me; and they *had* come for Francis.

6:12 PM.

Something toppled over and I cursed and spun and would have fired my gun if not for the safety being on. A storm of confused dust motes flung themselves every which way as a rat the size of Jörmungandr slithered snakelike across the Rowlings' desolate dinner table and found its way into the brick wall via secret passage. I cursed again and went up the stairwell, toward Hector Rowling's bedroom, where John R. Francis would have investigated if not for the cloaked, masked figure

(*macheteing*)

stopping him.

The stairs were unusually quiet for a place as old as this lighthouse. On a small landing between the first and second floor stood a small coffee table, abandoned in the lighthouse's dusty memory, with a seemingly empty vase atop. I looked inside and I saw two things. Not two separate things, mind you: rather two things at once, both occupying the same physical plane.

The psychic occupant of the vase was a dog head, bloomed roses where eyes should have been. I blinked and it was gone; I chalked it up to raw nerves. The temporal occupant of the vase, however, was merely a spider in a web. It was consuming another spider: a Goliath-predator compared to its David-prey: another Bible story I somehow knew through cultural osmosis.

My feet felt funny as I walked the rest of the stairs to the handsome but time-worn mezzanine. Legs felt like spider stalks, and I had a bizarre, irrational fear as I brought my gun and phone/flashlight up to my face that someone had pulled off my *other* two arms and two legs. Phantom pain coursed through my body and soul, stemming from a false idea that I was (trust me when I say it sounds as crazy to me admitting I had this thought—*belief*—as it certainly does to you) a mutilated arachnid.

I blinked and breathed in and remembered I was human.

"*Ishmael*," I muttered, not knowing what Ishmael meant nor where it came from.[10]

Clara Rowling's room lay before me, its door as open as it had been for John R. Francis. I stepped inside. *Briefly.* The thought of what heinous acts the killer had inflicted upon the ten-year-old girl—an innocent youth, a girl who collected all things My Little Pony[11], whose room I now stood in as a secular trespasser against her spectral commemoration—melted my stomach into sour mush. It felt profane to have kept her kiddish horsey dolls the way they were.

They kept them here, an almost audible voice whispered, *in case she comes back.*

I cursed, backed away, and unintentionally made the same drunken U-turn as Francis had made toward what had to have been Hector's room.

---

[10] He is the first son of the Bible's Abraham, but there's no way I would have known that (cultural osmosis or otherwise). More likely than not, I'd seen some *Moby Dick* adaptation on TV. Ishmael is the name of the protagonist.

[11] Yeah, *I know.* The flash drive. But it hadn't crossed my mind at the time of journaling about this event.

6:20 PM.[12] *Still* plenty of time (or so I thought).

I shone the light inside Hector's bedroom. There was no silhouette before the window. No hollow-eyed death-face staring back at me. But things squirmed at the edges of my light where the almost-palpable melancholy ate the glow; the bedroom's darkness seemed to be teeming with life. With . . . *fish.* Their never-blinking eyes like piercing voids. And I thought they were some-how—and for some reason—challenging me, but every time I washed my light across these areas, the *nightfish* would hurriedly swim away.[13]

Then I entered Hector's room.

John R. Francis was (probably) murdered because of something in this room. That's why the cloaked figure had stood in his way. That's why another cloaked figure had been there to block his escape. That's why the van was there to run him down if he'd been lucky enough or

---

[12] When I got back to the inn—*much later* than I was expecting, which you'll later understand why—I transferred my phone's footage to my MacBook and discovered that I had stared into that vase for a few seconds over five minutes. Considering what was streaming through my blood, and the ever-prowling, skulking, fucking-forward momentum of 7 PM., I count myself lucky.

[13] Also, upon revisiting this footage on my MacBook, I discovered I kept on repeating "Ishmael" like a mantra. I never captured any definite footage of the *nightfish*—the footage was too pixelated—but I promise you they were there. I'm not crazy.

skilled enough to have absconded from his attackers.

The *nightfish* seemed to whisper from Hector's closed closet door as if there were an unspoken contract—that my ignoring them (or having a source of light) would result in their leaving me alone. The phone's light burned holes in the dark nooks and crannies. The gun felt like thirty pounds. I was suddenly very tired, noticeably woozy, and that's when I saw it.

A heavy-duty safe tucked in the room's corner—above it, from a wire fastened on a hook in the ceiling, hung a gaudily oversized fish-crucifix. My spidery stalk-legs took me across the room where they planted themselves firmly before the safe; screaming in severe psychic distress were my severed phantom-arachnid extremities.

I knelt down.

The safe was not quite the size of a gun cabinet, but larger than one might expect a young man to have in his room. Larger, in fact, than one might even expect the parents to have.

A combination padlock with three wheels—each containing nine digits—appropriately halted my progress.[14]

------

[14] While the details of the my recent dream/hallu-cination were still at that moment, standing there in front of the safe, fresh and vivid (a storm full of strange phantasmagorias, alien concepts, and false memories raging in my head, threatening to perhaps erase my own identity, my own *existence*), it didn't occur to me to attempt the numbers 324 given to me by the woman at the bar in the manuscript in my dream/hallu-cination . . . because why would it? I *had* met a woman at *The Fish Tavern*, who, on the city council, was "high

6:23 PM.

The *probatio* may very well have been in that thick, immovable safe (yes, I was desperate enough to try), but access to it was verboten. From my haunches I lowered myself into a cross-legged position and studied the shape and material of what might as well have been an enigmatic monolith in a faraway land—black, cold-looking, and maddeningly incomprehensible. I flashed the cone of light through the darkness of the room, casting away the gloomy unknownness from every nook and cranny, until I felt comfortable enough to set down the gun and lean back on my—

Molten fire sizzled from my hand up to my elbow. I cursed and dropped my phone. Darkness descended upon the room, swallowing every trace of light except for the feeble illumination leaking through the partially boarded-up bedroom window. The flickering beams danced amidst the stagnant air, casting distorted shadows upon the decaying walls. Opaque tension filled the room. Then a sound. I stood confused as to the *growling* on the floor. Irrational fears coiled like serpents, their venomous fangs striking at the edges of my fragile sanity and extracting *form* from *void* and molding it into the Jörmungandrat from the living quarters who fled into the walls, and its ambiguous nature strobed redly and hotly behind my anxiety-paralyzed eyes: a kaleidoscope of nightmarish imaginings. Even the *nightfish* fled its predatory snarl.

---

up" (her words, likely to take me home, for she was clearly of the desperate variety, observably lonely, and very, very drunk). I don't actually remember her name and had saved her number as "Drunk Lady."

Each time the Jörmungandrat growled, I noticed the edges of my face-down phone would glow. That's when my senses returned in a calming wave and I snatched up my phone (same unknown number), pushed answer, and pressed it to my ear.

"*Is this Felix?*" Still a whorl of voices in the background, but less chaotic—as if the party was dwindling down.

"Yeah, who am I speaking to? Is this John?" (As in John R. Francis, the idea having unexpectedly jumped into my brainpan.)

From under the bed I could see the *nightfish* checking to see if the

(*ghost*)

coast was clear.

"*Detective Washington.*" His voice cut through the air, and for some reason Denzel Washington's face superimposed itself onto the man's voice.

I sauntered across the room, fixing my gaze on the window-slats, peering through them

(*they come like clockwork after 7*)

like an anxious voyeur trying to catch another voyeur spying on me. Perhaps the *they* about whom the drunk woman texted me were the cops after all. Maybe the safe was a trap and they were staking out the lighthouse to see if someone came to revisit the crime scene like some serial killers do, or pyromaniacs who watch from afar and jack off to their fiery handiwork. But I couldn't see anyone, and I'd parked far enough from the lighthouse as not to draw any attention. Plus, there was a public park and walking trail not too far away. Nothing stirred out there.

"*Hello?*" Him.

"Yeah?" Me.

"*Can you hear me?*"

"I think so."

"*Umm, yeah, sure, okay. Listen, Felix . . . do you have a last name?*" I didn't answer, yet he carried on as if my silence hadn't existed. "*I need you to come down to the morgue at your earliest convenience. We have a body. It's Brian Maxwell, we believe.*"

"What? Maxwell, he's dead? I just spoke with him."

I shouldn't have said that.

I turned around, glimpsing a *nightfish* inching its way toward my ankle before seeing that I saw it seeing me—

It recoiled and darted back under the bed and glanced my way disdainfully.

"Fuck you," I whispered to it.

"*Come again?*" the detective inquired, which made me think again of the hypothetical pyromaniac, which then summoned images of the ominous cloaked figures, which finally evoked a plethora of profoundly disagreeable scenarios (some of them involved naked men with fish heads and raging erections—don't ask).

"Sorry, I wasn't talking to you; I was conversing with the fish . . . never mind. You know what I mean. Listen, Maxwell is—*was*—my employer."

"*Uh huh,*" said the voice. That *uh huh* could have meant two very different things, depending on if he was *Titans* Washington or *Training Day* Washington. "*How about this: you get your goddamn mother fucking ass to the morgue. I'll give you an address—but you sound young, so you can probably tell your phone to bring you here.*"

An image of King Kong on the Empire State Building flashed before my eyes, and I whispered—to which I'm sure he heard but didn't respond—"*Training Day,*" although he did kind of sigh.

"I'm not a family member, so why would you need

me to identify him? The only thing I can think of is that"—my wind of assertiveness abruptly melted away, my voice cracked, and the next three words were a question—"I'm a *suspect*?"

It felt like a week-long pause.

Until the detective laughed. "*Nah, you're not a suspect.*"

"I'm not?"

"*Ain't no way a man did what was did to Crazy Maxie, if you catch my drift. He was bit through, torn apart. So unless you're a shark, or maybe even a quarter shark, you're not a suspect. Why? Would you like to be one?*"

"A shark?"

"*A suspect.*" He paused. "*Now listen. Crazy Maxie's closest family members are not . . . I think the best word—no, the* kindest *word—well, they're not reliable. Must run in the family. The closest relative is in the loony bin, and the* most *reliable one lives in Oregon—a cousin twice removed or something. She hasn't seen him since they were kids. And, as it is, Felix—you were the only goddamn person saved on his phone. But it sounds like you're under the influence, so you might not be fucking reliable either. Are you reliable?*"

I had to think about it.

"I'm reliable."[15]

---

[15] I wasn't.

IN REALMS ETHEREAL, where shadows entwine,
  Their minds pirouette with spectral bliss,

As if a corpse rejoices in festivity,
  Within the theatre macabre, their thoughts persist,

Chains of axioms shattered, they ascend,
  Beyond the mortal guise, their true form revealed,
  An allegiance forged amidst the abyss's **abyss**[16].

---

[16] Charlie Blackwood's entire manuscript (not to be confused with his discovered journal)—what we call *The Second Book of Jonah*—is still in mint condition to this day. However, only one word in the entire preserved gospel is of a compromised nature. Many Vicars and High Fishes have debated over this one word. While no one of us can know the inspired word for a certainty, the scholars of many generations have settled for "abyss" as only because it is the preceding word, and thus not adding any new meaning. The intention of "abyss's abyss" is only to neutralize controversy. Although

Night, maternal and eldritch, the womb,
    Where secrets gestate in ethereal gloom.
And in their surrender, a sacred rite,
    We, the Dag Elohim, welcome their flight,

Unraveling the tapestry of mortal flesh,
    Awakening the slumbering fish, esoteric and fresh,

Within the abyss lies the essence they seek,
    The essence of being, profound and oblique.

---

it should be mentioned that many believe that the
damaged word had been **"wives."**

QUESTION: IS THE "SECOND BOOK OF JONAH" THE INSPIRED WORD OF GOD?

ANSWER:

IT'S IMPORTANT TO FIRST UNDERSTAND that the US-originated *Second Book of Jonah* was written many centuries after the resurrection of Christ, as is also true with *The Book of Mormon*. While the passage of time and the location of authorship—not to mention the prose style, titanic word-count, and narrative structure—do not innately *disprove* its authenticity, it certainly does draw critical scrutiny unto itself.

But let's first look at a few of its strong claims.

The Second Book of Jonah has codes in the text that are comparable to the "Bible Code mania" of the late 90s and early 2000s. What this means is that, as in the Hebrew-written Tanakh, events that were unknown at the time of authorship can be found via particular numerical patterns. For example, if you take every seventh letter starting at chapter 7, verse 7, it spells out "united brothers fight brothers," which Fish Church believers argue means the Civil War; or even if it doesn't mean exactly that, its coherency—not to mention the numerical theme revolving around "7"—might nonetheless mean divine coding. Or starting with the twenty-eighth letter in *The Second Book of Jonah,* chapter 49, verse 1, and from there taking the twenty-seventh letter, the twenty-sixth, then the twenty-fifth letter, etc., the sentence it spells out is "the twins taste ash and blood." Again, believers argue this prophecy means the collapse of the World Trade Center.

However, the counterargument posed by some scholars—not dissimilar to criticisms journalist Michael Drosnin received for his book *The Bible Code* (1997)—is the "found prophecies" are so vague in nature that they can almost mean *anything*; and there's no way to disprove such messages weren't deliberately implanted, perhaps to give the illusion of divinity. Another counterargument: given that *any* book is long enough, readers, if they look hard enough, *will* find coincidental phrases—e.g., Herman Melville's *Moby Dick.* And as alluded to earlier, regarding canon consistencies, Charles Blackwood's *The Second Book of Jonah*'s word count is 80,000 words (on the nose, curiously enough). In comparison, scholars note that the New Testament is composed of 27 books, altogether 184,600 words—the longest being the book of Luke, with 19,482 words. Now of course *Moby Dick* is longer—206,052 words—with less "accidental prophecies" than *The Second Book of Jonah.* While most scholars and theologians will agree that the Tanakh and Bible codes are (probably) coincidental, many believe *The Second Book of Jonah* codes are deliberately embedded—crafted with enough ambiguity so as to gain credibility when future events appear to align with them.

Another common claim is that there are "overt prophecies" depicted. Chapter 42, verse 1-3, presents the most controversial one:

> *"Perchance, in days to come, that gentleman— yea, that wayfarer who unknowingly traverses the lingering remembrance of a Solitary Great Dreamer—shall chance upon thy melody. He shall find himself within one of the scant extra-holy crossroads upon this land, a solitary hotel; a barren expanse of firm, rugged, scorching ebony stone that enshrouds it, where metallic chariots come to rest; baked by a crimson sun or moon or eye. And perchance, the gentleman shall behold thy visage through a casement in a chamber."*

The argument is that Blackwood is describing (1) a modern hotel, (2) a parking lot, (3) motor vehicles, and that (4) "thy visage through a casement in a chamber" means watching a TV in a room.

However, we must look at *The Second Book of Jonah* as a whole to assess its authenticity. The first thing to point out is that Christ Jesus never appears in the text—unlike in *The Book of Mormon*—except for the possible mentioning of Him in chapter 42, verse 13: "he who proclaims the number of the YHWH Fish at the throat of the inviolate structure, at the **darkhouse** where thy broods had flourished for eons, and from the gullet shall thy wind-song be sung and hearkened, and he who uttereth that extraholy three digits shall be Swallowed until the day of Divine Judgment. So be it. Amen."

Critics bring up this point: if it was in reference to Christ, Blackwood had failed to capitalize the "h" in "Him"—therefore immediately disqualifying its canon in the New Testament. Likewise, if it wasn't about Christ Jesus, then *The Second Book of Jonah* mentions Him not one time. However, it's the usage of the word "YHWH" and "Elohim" that is most insightful as to the text's strange thought-origins: that of the Jewish Tanakh.

It's only when we take a deeper look into the history of ▮▮▮▮▮▮▮ that you get a stronger sense of this late 17th century apocryphal work. Most Christian and Jewish scholars look to the two figures closest to Blackwood. The first being one of the town's elders, Eberlein Grayson, who was the father of ▮▮▮▮▮▮▮'s "founding father," Fredrick Grayson—a Messianic Jew (in fact, a rabbi who converted to Eastern Orthodoxy and became a priest) who was also well-versed in Hebrew. The second being his wife, Alma Rowling, whom some scholars believe partook in an early variant of Wicca, while others speculate it was an obscure pagan religion lost to us. The latter argument, pertaining to her innate influence over her husband Charles Blackwood, may explain certain repeated occult-leaning phrases—neither of the Christian or Jewish canon nor of Wiccan terminology—throughout *The Second Book of Jonah*: "Solitary Great Dreamer," "Dag Elohim," "Five Anteriors," "The Dream of the Five Orbs"; not to mention names of beings of angelic stature (though not explicitly termed "angels"—fallen or otherwise): Grom, Draguana, Rust, Cabala, and Oslo; and also a slew of "Lesser Offspring" (never referenced as Nephilim): Dag Elohim (a Child of the Abyss/Oslo), Torlos (an Emissary of Draguana the Fallen One), the Weavers (Cabala's "divided form"), and the Gardeners (Broods of Rust).

While an imaginative optimist may view these five beings as fallen angels, and their offspring as Nephilim, we must acknowledge that the narrative of *The Second Book of Jonah* isn't consistent with the nature, actions, and attitude of God. And as the book seems to carry on the narrative style and some terms from the Old Testament (chiefly "YHWH" and sometimes, more to the Jewish tradition, "Elohim"), it fails to be Christ-centric.

One likely reason for this religion's creation may be a permutation of the desperation and hunger of the ex-communicated pilgrims in contrast to Charles Black-wood's native inclination to fulfill the role of a charis-matic leader. To go one step further, it's speculated that the "Sea Manna" (scarcely-researched marine organ-isms whose protection stems from laws influenced by religious practices) may have produced some psyche-delic effects when consumed, especially in such a deeply fasted state.

It's important to understand that even Satan—as de-tailed in the books of Matthew, Mark, and Luke—was well-versed in Scripture when he tried to tempt Jesus after His forty-day fast; so if some of the prophecies in *The Second Book of Jonah* seem tantalizingly true, in the Old Testament even the Pharaoh's magicians were able to conjure serpents to compete with Moses's God-bestowed powers. The Adversary is not an inactive agent nor is he feeble. But as Matthew 7:16 says—"Ye shall know them by their fruits. Do men gather grapes of thorns, or figs of thistles?"

JOURNAL (V)

Somehow I had materialized in my car.

6:45 PM and I swore at this unexpected passage of time, glanced out the window, and saw a black van parked behind me. It was a public park (I wasn't naïve or irrational to the fact that some people simply had black vans), but, since it was winter and dark, I remember thinking: *Why the fuck is someone still at the park?*

Shortly after thinking that, I saw a woman and two little boys cross the street and enter the van.

My phone buzzed.

Maxwell was calling.

6:55 PM.

But I was already driving. Undernourished, serpentine trees lined the road like upward-rupturing intestines of some long-ago-interred god. Amidst this spectral panorama I thought I heard the swell and crashing of waves and, from the same direction, a storm of cicadas.[17] The scent of brine in the air mixed with sulphur. My windows down. Blood on my shirt. Was I on my way to the morgue? There were no GPS coordinates glowing

---

[17] It didn't occur to me till much later that cicadas would neither be making such a racket in winter, nor would they reside in the ocean.

in the dark. What was I doing? Where was my phone? Hadn't Maxwell called? And wasn't Maxwell dead? What and when and where and how?

Behind me I saw two things at once (not so different from looking into the vase on the stairwell landing, where I saw both dog head and spider), and as I write this I am not sure which one of these things I *really* saw, for both entity/object simultaneously manifested themselves with such vividness, coexisting within the confines of temporal confluence: a colossal ebony shark hovering above the sandy road, its eyes glowing dully crimson from my left taillight (left eye glowing a little brighter because my right one had burnt out), and also a black van driving slowly, its muted headlights dully reflecting my not-burnt-out taillight—and the moon, and the stars.

I drove into one of the dead god's intestines and felt glass and rough, piney-scented bark slap and scratch my face; I wondered how it had gotten into the middle of the road until I realized my car had somehow swerved between two palm trees and had gotten into a field where a very lonely willow wasn't so lonely anymore. Somehow I was lying on my back, branches swaying above me, breaking up the vista of misaligned and too-large stars and other, stranger bodies of cosmic madness; when I turned my head I saw the shark snarling and then I blinked and saw two van doors open and two figures get out, one carrying a machete. When I looked up, laughing, I saw a normal night sky. My car was smoking against the tree, bumper caved in. A spot of blood against the bark. My fingers found my mashed face and I said, "*Oh.*"

The

(*shark opened its eyes*)

van cast forth its headlights, which pierced through

the murky shadows and found their mark within the recesses of my hapless eyes. Two silhouettes stood before

> (*the eyes of*
> *the ghost of*
> דָּג אֱלֹהִים)

it, engulfed by the red-white glow. I tried to scoot away, my fingers digging into the sand-gritted grass. I kept stumbling, right arm rebelling against my efforts (broken, I later learned at the hospital), and I looked up and saw—straining my eyesight to its limits against the mingling of perfect-void blackness and blinding light—both figures had what looked like roses blossoming from the hollow eyes of their moldering, vaguely lupine faces. Both were snarling at me. One had a machete ready to swing, and the other carried a miniature mad scientist's lab: a syringe, a beaker, things I didn't have names for—

—a door opened—

—two more eyes cut through the dark, their stare fighting against the red-white supergaze of the

> (*shark*)

van and—

"—*FREEZE, FUCKERS!*"

I knew the voice.

An incalculable stretch of night separated me from Detective Washington. He walked into his own headlights, but since he was at an angle and I wasn't quite blinded by his headlights, I saw—and felt a superficial dismay to find—a middle-aged man, moderately overweight, balding, sporting a gloriously thick brown mustache. He wore a Hawaiian shirt tucked into beige cargos neatly rolled up at the cuffs, revealing white socks descending to beach sandals. He was also very white.

But his fashion choices weren't what held my attention; it was the really big magnum revolver he had to hold with two hands.

He fired.

The bullet struck Machete Man in such a way so as to dislodge his face—his *mask*—which whirled into the night that swallowed it. Invisible strings of force lifted him off the ground and he landed with his limbs sprawled out, which made him look like he'd been flash-frozen while doing face-down snow angels. And in a twist of almost ironical fate, the machete—after it loosed from his grip—would have speared my groin had I not quickly rolled away because I thought a five-inch spider was crawling on my chest (it was only a crab . . . I think).

The Mad Scientist, first seeing his gun-shot accomplice (not quite dead, I realized; he began flailing like a fish gasping for air) and then processing the mustachioed man with the really big magnum, dropped his medical stuff and frenetically ran toward where several trees pressing from low dunes regurgitated from their bases bone-white sand as if guardians to the beach beyond them.

Detective Washington grumbled a curse and crossed in front of me, his movements precise, and triple-tapped the Machete Man—once in his head, and once in the center of his back as if shooting him in the head wasn't good enough.

Then swiftly resetting the hammer, he took aim at the fleeing Mad Scientist, now crossing into some liminal space neither field nor beach—the detective pulled the trigger, the revolver boomed, the man fell.

A flicker of satisfaction danced across the detective's face, indicating his contentment with the accuracy of his shot; and as his focus turned toward me, I wondered for some reason if he was going to shoot me next—I mean, it wasn't like I was thinking rationally or anything. My vision kept cutting in and out—

The stars appeared extracosmic and insane, then concealed by clouds. Shark then van then shark then van again. *Training Day* Denzel Washington then off-brand Josh Brolin. Most absurdly, however, was the woman-shaped shadow standing behind the face-down Machete Man; shadow so completely black and solid that it would have looked like oil if not for its flickery, ephemeral nature, as if it couldn't quite find the right frequency to allow me to perceive it, to be born. Looking straight at me with pupilless eyes—

She said something.

I didn't hear her voice—I *felt* it. Except what I felt wasn't a voice. It was the shape of the words—no—the shape of the words' meaning—as if metaphysical parasites traversed into my mind from the invisible byway that connected her bone-white eyes to mine and carved into my mind the words: *His face will guide you.*

"Whose face?" I asked.

Detective Washington said, "What the fuck are you babbling about?"

His voice sounded underwater and far away.

A stench of sulphur and brine surfed the wind, and I gagged.

The woman made a movement. Her arm extended. Moonlight briefly revealed to me that her hand—her entire body—wasn't black because shadows had fashioned her; she was black because death had blackened her, disintegrated her, distended her, deformed her— death *became* her. I realized she was pointing her too-long finger to the Machete Man.

"*His* face?"

The metaparasites etched YES into my brain. Then the night swallowed the dead woman: she was gone.

And therefore I crawled toward and eventually reached the triple-tapped figure, despite Detective

Washington's warning to "chill the fuck out, man—your fuckin' arm's broken," getting blood all over my clothes as I drunkenly, irrationally, one-handedly tried to roll over the corpse so I could identify him—but I was tripping balls, and I felt like Mike Tyson had tied by feet with rope and strung me upside down and beat the brains out of my head . . . so I wasn't thinking clearly, okay? It never crossed my mind until about thirty seconds of what the detective must have observed as insanity to the nth degree that I could simply roll over top of the dead man and look at his face from the other side. (I did just that—yet it was harder to do than you might think.)

What remained of the museum volunteer's face stared back at me.

But, instead of expressing this revelation through my face or words, I turned to the detective and said (my mouth apparently operating on its own agenda): "I thought you were like me," meaning black, but then my eyes rolled back. I saw and heard nothing except for a milky void and disembodied voices . . .

I OPENED MY EYES AND found myself on a stiff hospital bed.

"Mr. Lucky awakens," said an older woman's voice. The nurse. But I don't know why but she looked like a long-distance runner who smoked too much. She'd been fiddling around with stuff on a tray before she glanced and smiled and spoke to me. Then she turned back around and began to re-fiddle.

"Where am I?" A taste of ash in my mouth.

"Hospital." Without turning around.

"Which one?" I tried to discretely spit out the taste, but only white foam came out. The nurse turned and wiped off my mouth and chin. She said:

"███████ Hospital. You've been in and out of consciousness for—has it been two days? No, three days."

"*Three?*"

I felt like she wanted to say *Did I stutter?* But instead she turned around and grabbed something from the visitor chair. A newspaper. She handed it to me, said "This one's local" as if there were others that weren't. The headline read: INTOXICATED JOURNALIST SURVIVES THE IMPOSSIBLE.

"Intoxicated?"

She looked at me funnily like we shared an uncomfortable secret.

"What?"

Come on, her face said. Then her mouth said, "It was in your system."

"What was?"

Again the *come on.* "You know you're lucky to be alive from the car accident alone. But you're a bit of a celebrity because of the *other thing.* You *did* make national news. CNN had a thing on you."

"The fuck you say?"

Come on.

"Sorry, ma'am."

That's better. "It might've been funny, really, if it hadn't been for the fact you'd almost died—twice. But I suppose some people *do* find it funny, don't they, even if they don't say it, and that's why it's become so popular. What is wrong with our world?" She sighed. "The doctor will be with you shortly."

She left and I read the paper.[18]

---

[18] I've found a copy online and included it for you to read. The file name is inventively titled "article."

THE DAGWOOD JOURNAL

INTOXICATED JOURNALIST SURVIVES THE IMPOSSIBLE
—by Ralph Margo Stovington

"AT FIRST I DIDN'T KNOW how to make heads or tails of the reports I heard last night," local fisherman Tom Wakemore says as he makes his morning errands to the post office and bakery. He'd been the first at the scene and immediately called the police. "Truth be told, I kind of felt as though kids were up at the shore blowing off fireworks, and I was ready to do to them on their heads what their fathers should be doing more frequently," he jests with a *thumping* gesture: knuckles against open palm. "But I suppose something felt off this morning. Red sky, moon still out, the waves eerily calm except for something or some*things* thrashing out there. A strange sort of melancholy fell on me. Already had my phone out before driving around the bend, I recall, but I don't know why except I guess for a hunch or something . . . and seeing what I saw . . ." Mr. Wakemore shakes his head, stares off into the sunset drifting down past the Great Fast memorial. He stays like this for a while. Then he says, "Sent chills through me. I thought a terrible car accident had happened by the way the bodies were scattered about the wreckage, and the man—the survivor—lying there, [blood] all over his face. I'd thought he'd had his head caved in with a baseball bat."

Police have since identified the injured man as journalist Felix Trellis and have taken him to ▮▮▮▮▮▮ Hospital, where doctors are treating his wounds.

"Traces of psilocin were found in his bloodwork, which may account for the car accident," police chief Brody O'Connor comments. "We're still looking into what happened to the other bodies. No further questions at this time."

I TRIED TO GET THE nurse to come back into the room, I tried "ma'am" and "nurse lady" and "miss" and "missus." Then I tried the buzzer and another nurse came in: a pretty, petite Hispanic girl who reminded me too much of an ex-girlfriend from college, which at once made me distrust her.

"Miss," I said, holding up the news article. "Question."

She nodded her head, waiting.

I opened my mouth to ask her what was going on; to tell her the article was grossly inaccurate; but perhaps, since I knew she didn't have the answers, what came out instead was a yawn.

She told me, "The doctor will be with you shortly, sir, and then you can leave."

"Leave?"

"Yeah huh." With birdlike movements she coasted into the hallway.

I sat there on the hospital bed.

Thinking.

Maxwell dead, but still he called.

Phone missing.

Detective Washington's Germanic whiteness (petty, I know, but still couldn't get over it).

The article's tilt.

Somehow being a celebrity all the sudden.

Rita Rowling's bloodstain on the ground in the hallway in the lighthouse. That weird dream or hallucination or prophecy, about a deep-sea chasm with my children who were for some reason crabs, about a manuscript called *The Swallowed Town*. Then reading from it, which triggered a dream within a dream within a—

Psilocybin.

"I was tripping balls," I said aloud.

Then again I thought of Detective Washington and his mustache, the ebony shark/black van/what-the-fuck-ever I saw out there near the beach, the Festival of the Fish . . .

There was something there, in the dark, in the cruelly unlit abyss of this mystery, something just beneath my fingertips, perhaps even brushing against them, and all I had to do was grip onto it, work it in my hand, discern its grooves in the nightlands of the unknown. Identify it. Prove it.

"Prove Hector's innocence," I muttered just as the door opened and a thirty-year-old doctor came in, explaining to me that he had to "make this real quick," so he made me touch my nose, stand up and touch my toes, and open up and say "ahhh." All the while I was trying to find a kink in his pretentious and completely narcissistic tongue-wagging armor to ask about the news article, but he kept talking. He then, of course not shutting up, jotted something on a piece of paper (my script) and said—yes, he actually said—"You're very lucky, dude. Next time don't party so hard and don't drive high. You should set up an appointment with your PCP to have your cast removed, or go to any urgent care if you're in a bind for time, as I am right now. Have a good day—

"Hey"—he snapped his fingers—"you're a writer, yeah—?"

I opened my mouth to say *yeah* but didn't get a chance to.

"—maybe you've got a novel in there." He tapped his skull. "About what happened. Oh and your friend is waiting outside."

"My friend?" he graciously allowed me to ask, but just shrugged and left and closed the door. I sat there baffled. The nurse stayed behind, briefly, like a reluctant shadow. Her face said *He is,* in response to my face asking *is he always a complete narcissistic asshole?* Behind her stood a large guy with tribal tattoos, a goatee, a manbun[19]; seeing him in hospital attendant scrubs dismayed me, and I was even more dismayed— *terrified*, really—to see his football player hands gripping the push handles of a wheelchair.

"I don't need that," I said, setting down the newspaper.

The nurse said, "It's policy. Javi will take care of you."

And indeed Javi took care of me. Pushed me an anticlimactic forty paces from the room to the front door that, in keeping with the outdatedness of ███████, wasn't even automated. An old man walking in with flowers held open the door for us. I nodded at the old man but the old man just winked at me.

---

[19] I can't remember if he'd been standing there the entire time, or if he'd recently entered the room. Noticing him startled me, though (I jumped—just a smidge), and I wasn't convinced he was real until he started pushing me. And even then . . . I had doubts.

"Dare you ah, man," said the booming thunder behind me. I stood up, my arm a dully throbbing mush in my cast. And Javi ambled back into the small hospital, the now-vacant wheelchair squeaking in front of him.

It took me a moment to orient myself.

Even then, I half expected to find John R. Francis—maybe with a small posse of pink- or blue-haired groupies, all with the newest iPhone in their hands, necks bent uncomfortably low—standing in front of a Tesla, cocky grin on his face. Instead I found a gaudy station wagon from the Stone Age and a white man leaning against it, aviator sunglasses hiding his eyes. Toothpick in mouth. Folded, hairy arms. You know the stance—you've seen it in a hundred different movies.

Strolling forward, I said (half joking), "Do you still need me to identify Maxwell?"

And picking his teeth, he said (very seriously), "I do. He's in a fridge. They're *all* in a fridge."

~~110~~	~~125~~	~~140~~	~~155~~	~~170~~
~~111~~	~~126~~	~~141~~	~~156~~	~~171~~
~~112~~	~~127~~	~~142~~	~~157~~	~~172~~
~~113~~	~~128~~	~~143~~	~~158~~	~~173~~
~~114~~	~~129~~	~~144~~	~~159~~	~~174~~
~~115~~	~~130~~	~~145~~	~~160~~	~~175~~
~~116~~	~~131~~	~~146~~	~~161~~	~~176~~
~~117~~	~~132~~	~~147~~	~~162~~	~~177~~
~~118~~	~~133~~	~~148~~	~~163~~	~~178~~
~~119~~	~~134~~	~~149~~	~~164~~	~~179~~
~~120~~	~~135~~	~~150~~	~~165~~	~~180~~
~~121~~	~~136~~	~~151~~	~~166~~	~~181~~
~~122~~	~~137~~	~~152~~	~~167~~	~~182~~
~~123~~	~~138~~	~~153~~	~~168~~	~~183~~
~~124~~	~~139~~	~~154~~	~~169~~	

I'm glad you've kept up with these journals, Felix. Feeling any better?

I'm not so sure if "better" is the right word. But sure, let's say I'm better.

Then how do you feel? I mean, since journaling?

Well, I've *always* journalized my work. I'm a journalist, remember. In fact, I'd been keeping a journal since last year. I wrote it all down after... you know... what had happened.

And does your, umm, let's say "contemporary memory" of events line up with what had actually happened?

I don't know. I think so. But I don't know.

[a beat]

It's like my mind has been divided ever since... being drugged. I keep on having dreams about the manuscript.

Would you like more coffee, hon, before continuing?

Yes, ma'am.

Let me text Sam out in the lobby. Hang on. [*tapping*] **There.**

[*footfalls*]

You don't hear that? Sounds like wind.

Uh-uh. You said you hear *wind*?

Yeah, like, wind through a... never mind. That's a name of a Stephen Ki... Doesn't matter. Sounds like a strong wind pushing through a small space.

A vacuum cleaner?

No.

[door opens, footfalls, "half and half and a stevia"]

Thank you, Sam. We ended our last session by talking about the hospital. You were brought outside in a wheelchair. They released you. Then what

happened?

Detective Washington picks me up from the hospital. My car is wrecked. Lost my phone. So he takes me to the morgue. Police are pretty persistent about this whole identifying-the-body thing. Even though he *knew* what Maxwell looked like because of both of them being ███████ locals.

I remember a strange cloud formation over the morgue. It's like... even the sky knows this place is full of sorrow and doesn't want to disrespect our feelings, however insignificant they are in the grand scheme of things; and maybe I was thinking that *because* of the accidental therapeutic aftereffects of the psilocybin, too; who knows? So yeah. It's dark and gloomy and Detective Washington walks ahead of me and holds open the morgue door as I make my way up the shadow-engulfed sidewalk — like some kid got carried away with a gray crayon: I remember thinking that; remember also thinking that whatever door the psychedelic trip at the lighthouse had opened, I could — as the doctor halfheartedly joked about — actually write a novel about it. Or at least a fucking good article to prove Hector Rowling's innocence. Language, I'm bad I know. I'm sorry. Anyway.

So I follow the white man.

Why white?

Why indeed.

[*laughter*] **What? No, I mean, why are you specifying his being Caucasian?**

I suppose I never mentioned this in our earlier sessions — but in the lighthouse, when he first called me, I imagined him being black. Like... in my mind's eye or whatever.

Did he *sound* black? And can't a white person sound like me and you?

[*a beat*] Sure, I guess. But no. I mean, you can just *tell*, you know? Anyway, Detective Washington, I guess he sounded more like... Josh Brolin... and somehow I misidentified him... stereotyped him... cigarette-y gruff, crunchy-voiced. I think it was only his last name that made me think he was a brother.

What? [*a beat*] ***Oh.***

So — okay, I gotta apologize in advance because in order to, um, *encapsulate the essence* of Detective Washington, I gotta cuss. A lot.

Say anything you'd like, Felix.

Okay. Well, we go into the basement. It's weird how silent it is — no tv, no radio, no wind beating against the building. The all-consuming nothingness pressing in on us seems to even swallow our footsteps. We round the corner and he opens a door, nods for me to enter. I'm a little hesitant, you know. Like, what if Washington's hand slips as he's holding the door open for me and it closes between us and somehow locks and I'm trapped in there with this open-eyed corpse staring back at me? Irrational, I know, but I remember thinking it. A corpse *is* there, obviously, but not right in front of me; it's laid out on a tray, the kind you pull out from the wall. A sheet over it. There are three sheeted figures. A woman's in there, too. A *living* woman. She looks too... normal to be working at a morgue.

Detective Washington says, "We're here," as if the woman hadn't already been looking at us.

The woman is slender. I look at her ring finger but I'm dismayed to find that she's wearing gloves. I'd rather be on a date with her than looking at dead bodies — she never speaks as she waits for us to cross the morgue refrigerator. Once we're next to her, she pulls off sheet number one and Detective Washington says, "Well?"

"Well *what*?" I ask.

"Well, identify this fucker so we can get the fuck out of here."

I allow my eyes to drift to the macabre, ruined effigy. The detective was right. A human could not have done this to another human. The carnage from below the waist was too organically torn up, with teeth marks and everything, for it to be anything other than a shark attack. Or some other kind of marine animal. I look at the dead man's face and say, "That's not him."

He looks at me without speaking, his eyes huge. He

wants to say something, to cuss just to cuss: I see it in his eyes. He exchanges a glance with the silent woman. Her expression is indecipherable.

"When did you last see Maxwell? Maybe your memory's off."

"No," I tell him. "I met him just, what, yesterday? Or... however many days ago... before the hospital. The day that what happened had happened was the day I met him. The only time I *ever* met him. At his house. And I remember being a little surprised looking at him because of how his voice sounded on the phone."

"How so?" His toothpick falls from his mouth but his deceptively dexterous hand catches it mid-fall; in one smooth motion he reinserts it between his scruffy lips.

"I just imagined he'd be taller, I guess."

"I'm not following."

"The man who let me in was the man I spoke to on the phone. I'm only saying I remember taking note of his short stature in juxtaposition to his big voice."

"Juxta-pah-what?"

"Nothing. My point is: the man I spoke to was about this tall" — I point at the corpse — "*with* legs"

"You're saying that that was the first time you met him, huh?" He hums, takes out his toothpick, studies it. Hums again. "Well, let me tell *you* something, man: this fella definitely *is* Brian Maxwell, but he's been in the belly of a shark for" — looking over to the mortician, who nods when he says — "two weeks. See the skin? Shark's stomach acid caused it to look this way. That and saltwater immersion. You know what

I'm trying to say, don't you?"

When I don't immediately answer, he spells it out for me that I probably never spoke to Maxwell — the *real* Maxwell — except for maybe when he initially hired me via email. And then, pretentiously placing the toothpick between his teeth and pointing with his other hand at the two other dead people, he says, "You know what these are?"

"Dead people," I offer.

"No," he says.

"No?"

"Well, yes. They *are* dead. Obviously. What I mean is, they're not *just* dead people; they're your infamous *muggers*. Let's see if my working theory is right." He nods to the mortician. Her normal eyes flicker to me in a way that silently and simultaneously asks me if I'm ready and assures me everything will be fine. Then she pulls the sheet away. I see the man. Naked. A hole in his head from Washington's really big magnum.

"You know this man?"

"I do," I say.

"Is he your Maxwell?"

"No," I say.

Then he says, "The hell you mean you know him but he's not your Maxwell?"

"He's a volunteer at the museum."

He cusses again and then pulls off the third sheet.

"This him?"

I look at the man. I shake my head no. Then I remember something. "Hey, shouldn't there be a fourth body?"

The detective and mortician exchange glances.

"The news article," I say. "Said there were three bodies other than my own."

"The driver," he says. "The family already identified him —"

"— and what's this stuff about *me* shooting them?"

"Okay, quiet down. We'll, um — thank you, ma'am, that'll be all for today — we'll talk about it. Come on. Let's get coffee."

And you know the rest of the story. Turns out, due to an ongoing investigation, the police fed false information to the guy who wrote the article; it made me famous in the process, so I can't complain.

Remember me saying the woman at the bar told me "they come like clockwork after seven"?

I do.

Apparently she meant a combination of "shady people" and "cop activity" after all. [*Laughter*] And there I was for the longest time imagining crab people, evil sirens, and persons with a certain "Innsmouth look" about them — obscure reference, never mind; turns out — for the longest time, since the Lighthouse Killings took place — neighbors had been calling the police, complaining about *strange activities*. You know. People wearing masks. Hoods. Entering the lighthouse through one of the half-boarded windows. So yeah, like I said, either the cops would come around nightfall — or the "shady people" would. Over and over again. Like —

— clockwork.

Was his name-o. Turns out Detective Washington had a working theory that complemented Hector's hypothetical innocence, although he didn't see the connection at the time.

You're talking about the safe?

Yes. The easiest pill to swallow would be the idea that a group of people wanted to burglarize any remaining items in the lighthouse, and that they only *accidentally* stumbled across a safe. Mind you, a safe with only three combination wheels. Zero through nine on each one. Only a thousand different combinations (yeah, I did the math). A daunting task, sure, but manageable — maybe they wanted a challenge, I don't know. I felt how heavy that safe is, Dr. Thawlen, and there is no way they'd be able to move it. It's so heavy it felt like it might as well have been bolted into the ground. Anyway. Even after the three people had tried to kill me, the detective hadn't connected the Hector-dots: meaning that the safe was the *entire* reason for the elaborate murders, along with pinning it on Hector, and somehow having Hector go along with it.

So we're now at a local breakfast restaurant even though it's eight p.m. "If they tried to kill me," I say to Detective Washington, "then what makes you think they didn't kill the Rowlings?"

"You really think they killed the family?"

"I do," I tell him.

He sips his coffee, looks out the window at the town's quaint nightlife, and says, "Well, we *did* find a journal with attempted combinations; maybe that could be enough to reopen the case, in terms of a motive."

That's how I found out about this journal — which, by the way, was one of the key pieces of evidence that eventually proved Henry's innocence. They also found fingerprints all over the house that matched each of the corpses at the morgue.

He gets out soon, doesn't he? I saw an article on Google. My phone probably knew I was having an appointment with you. You know how phones are.

He gets out next week. The antediluvian legal gears turning and all that jazz take a lifetime, it seems.

Sorry, I got you off track. Please continue. You were in the restaurant.

At that point, our conversation is pretty much over, but I do mention one thing to the detective... if opening the safe was really that important, why did they bother following me from the lighthouse? Because I *discovered* the safe? Why didn't they keep on trying to open it? I can only assume it's because I'd seen one of their faces when I was high. Anyway. After I say this, he hums thoughtfully and sips his coffee thoughtfully and says "At least we know there's at least one more of them out there" thoughtfully.

"I'm confused about that part," I tell him. "He's the one who gave me John R. Francis's flash drive" (I'd already told him about John R. Francis's own investigation when he drove me to the morgue). "He gave me extra money to continue the investigation. *He* did. Not the real Maxwell; rather, the fake one. Why didn't *he* — or *they* — just take the *real* Maxwell's money instead of giving it to me, *if* fake-Maxwell was one of them, and *if* they wanted money from the safe?"

"Maybe it's not money they're looking for," he says. "Maybe it's something more... profound. Did this *little man* want you to open the safe?"

"Never mentioned it."

He hums and starts tapping his finger.

And why did he spike my tea? It clearly wasn't to kill me. Otherwise it would have been poison. Unless... I don't know... he actually isn't one of them. If he isn't, then who is he?   I'm sorry, I'm babbling.

It's just... those puzzle pieces still don't fit, despite how much I've looked into it. I never found my phone or the gun fake-Maxwell had given me; maybe it had blanks, or maybe when I was high I'd fired at one of them, and that's why they followed me. The police never found fake-Maxwell's prints at Maxwell's house. Only real-Maxwell's prints. The man pretending to be him must have wiped them thoroughly. Either way, between the notebook with the attempted locker combinations, my testimony, not to mention my piece — those things were the catalysts for the retrial.

Here's the weird thing, though:

After my article, and shortly before the retrial, I call

the ███████ State Penitentiary because I wanted to set up a phone interview with him. With Hector Rowling. The person talking to me kind of sighs. Like this question had been asked a hundred times. I tell them this was different, and then the noise they give me is like, "Sure it is." He tells me Hector Rowling had said all there is to say on the topic of murdering his family.

"But I have evidence that he's innocent," I say.

Noise on the other end. It almost sounds like… never mind. You don't hear that, Dr. Thawlen? Sounds like sticking an ear up to a conch, but it's coming from somewhere over *there*—

There's nothing there, Felix. Did you ever get your phone interview?

He said he'd pull a few strings to allow me an interview with a cellmate. The caveat, though, was that the cellmate — a mister Yuri Reed — had a "phone-call phobia." Reed had the paranoid supposition that the person on the other end might not be who they said they were. "Might not in fact be human," the man on the phone told me. "So you'll have to be here in person."

I'm assuming you bought a plane ticket.

I've got a fear of planes.

I drove.

I was in too deep.

I guess when those people tried to kill me, it made

things personal. And mind you, fake-Maxwell was still out there and I... well, another reason I wanted to talk to Hector — in this case, his cellmate — was to get the bloody lock combination. To see if matched up with my... dreams.

[a long beat]

It takes me over four hours to get there. I stay at a dingy motel. There are cockroaches but I don't mind — when you survive the machinations of your own murder, you tend not to sweat the small stuff. I wash up, go to bed, fall asleep, and I find "The Swallowed Town" at the border of that void in my dream. And I fall into it. And in the manuscript in my dream, I *do* speak to Hector.

Dream-Hector confirms it.

324.

"Open it," he tells me. "It will make your dreams come true," he tells me. "You will see the face of God," he tells me.

So I go back to the lighthouse/darkhouse — in the manuscript, not the dream (even though the manuscript is in my dream... if that makes sense) — and I'm in awe of its... presence. It stands... disturbingly... in a canopy of low-hanging, overlarge stars and odder, less definable bodies of what I can only describe as "supermatter." An acquiescence washes over my mind as the tide washes over my feet, and as I walk I keep having the urge to duck. Because of the sky. How low it is. It's not like I'm afraid of bumping my head, no, but it's rather analogous to... walking down an old cobweb-infested cellar where eight-legged things crawl about unseen — I didn't know what was *up* there, Dr. Thawlen, what would brush against my head or shoulders. Anyway. So I hunker down, persevere, and enter the **darkhouse**.

The door is missing.

It's just an open chasm. Within its confounding depths, the very essence of lodestone pervades every aspect, as if enticement itself were wrenched from its intended course, bending to the whims of this enigmatic void inside the **darkhouse**; and I, an unwitting participant in its insidious design, find myself drawn by an invisible force, a quasi-magnetic compulsion, coerced to tread the path it dictated. And because the door is missing — had been for some unknowable timespan — there is exposed to me, upon entering the **darkhouse**, an interior brimming with an alarming assortment of lifeforms. On islands of twisted shadow against the interior are Jonah crabs, their shells in varying stages of decay, scuttling amidst bleak remnants; and seven-armed colossal starfish suicidally clinging to the walls and ceiling; and seagulls, bereft of wings and swollen beyond reason, bearing beaks elongated to monstrous proportions, mocking the natural order that had shaped them; and the *nightfish* are there, perpetually dwelling within ebony recesses; and too-black slugs or leeches and sizeable sea anemones and strangely moveless octopi, semitranslucent, occupying puddles formed in depressions on the floor.

Yet it's a ceaseless ballet of uncanny movement that triggers my anxiety. Scurrying nonstop through an elaborate maze of cordgrass, needlerush, bluestem, and other towering, invasive vegetative masses — some like fine-haired cucumbers blossoming with mad stuff, others not so describable — are what I initially mistook for long-legged crabs but are in fact massive kaleidoscopic arachnids, their form a shifting phantasmagoria.

And they all — all these things — all these organisms — all these floras — everyfuckingthing — have fruiting bodies. They'd infect me with their spores had I not been a *dream-passenger* merely reading from "The Swallowed Town." What I mean is that there was an *added layer of protection*, an extra bulwark between me and those... *things*.

So they let me pass. Then I woke up. Drove the rest of the way to ███████ State Penitentiary. Spoke to Yuri Reed.

Hmm. May I ask you something else, Felix?

I guess so.

I want to emphasize that there is no pressure whatsoever to decline this suggestion, and I genuinely believe that you may not *necessarily* require this particular course of action. However, in my professional opinion, your fixation with ████ ████'s history, the case, the imaginary "Swallowed Town" manuscript, and the traumatic experience you endured... frankly, it's swallowing you whole.

Delving deeper into your psyche through the process of hypnosis may be therapeutic for you, although

there is no guarantee of its efficacy. Yet gaining a
comprehensive understanding of this underlying low-
grade mania could aid others grappling with similar
stress-related disorders.

Are you willing to go to a session?

"COULD YOU PLEASE STATE YOUR name and your rela-tionship with Mr. Hector Rowling?"

"Yuri Reed. I'm, uh, Hector's roommate. I mean cell-mate, 'cause we's locked up in the slammer."

"Good. Thank you for finding time to speak with me, Mr. Reed."

A beat.

Material ruffles.

Clacking sound.

Chair squeals.

A thump.

"Are you okay?"

"When you called me 'Mr. Reed,' I got to thinkin maybe my daddy tagged along."

"Yuri, then?"

"Thah's my name, ain' it? An darlin, who might you be?"

"My name is Felix Trellis. I'm a writer—"

Chair squeals. Fingers tap tap tap.

"Oooh, are ya'll fixin for Hector to be a star in one of those—what do you call em—True Crime tales? You should get that Timothy Charmander feller. Young n tall n thin jus like my Hector."

"Unfortunately I'm not that kind of writer. I'm a

journalist."

"Well, I don' rightly see whah else yer aimin to wring outta me thah hadn' already by the others."

"Others?"

"Like yerself: Journalists."

"Are you always his spokesperson?"

"Nah at the beginnin. But lately I been. Sick n done of it all is whah he is. A sweet boy thah Hector, n he jus wanna be lef alone. He ain' sorry for wha he done, neither, if thah's whah yer askin."

"I'm sorry?"

"Yer sorrier than he is, then."

"No, I mean—listen, I've got evidence that he didn't kill his family."

Laughter.

"Well now, darlin, y'all done gah yuhself the wrong kind of evidence. Lemme tell yuh somethin, mister: I ain' sayin he a monster, I'm jus sayin his kinfolk sure were. At leas thah whah he believe. Claimed he'd do it all over again. Reckoned they was . . . well, too bad y'all ain' penning a book or something 'cause this here would be the juicies par, even if it's only make-believe. Gotta be, don' it?"

"I'm not sure unless you tell me."

"Way he spins it: They wasn' even human no more, his fam'ly. Nah really. Nah in the way yuh n I circumscribe humanity—yuh should use that word if yuh write abou this. I read it in a book some time ago."

"What do you mean 'they weren't even human?'"

A beat.

"Ya tell me, mister. Already told ya'll it's a fiction. Gotta be. But he did say they was once his fam'ly, before they were—I don't know. Forget the word he said. 'Miseries' or such. But he took an ax, then ya know whah he did? He axed em. Not a question, either.

"*Ya look mighty le'down, donchya? Might nah even believe me but yuh should. Evidence or nah, Hector doesn' wan' no leavin here.*"

A long beat.

A cough.

"*Why wouldn't he want to leave? If he's innocent? If it can be proven?*"

"*I like to believe is because of yers truly, but . . .*" *A sigh.* "*Says he n his children are waiting for him. To fu'fill somethin. Fam'ly tradition or condition or some such -ition; some such somethin. His blood is contractually needed, if yuh can believe tha.*"

"*Who's 'he and his children'?*"

A beat.

"*I think a priest. Or maybe his father.*"

"*His father's dead.*"

"*No; his real papa. I don't know, mister. Talks abou this Father Saccharine or some such name. If he's not his real daddy, he mus be related—you know, jus certain words he use. Can't remember off the top of my head. Ancestorial types of words.*"

A beat.

"*What I think is, his admitting to murder is a form of escapism.*"

"*Ya'll believe whah yuh wanna believe. Yer half-right though. Abou the escapism part.*"

A knocking sound.

"*Well, looks like our time's grown legs n run out on us—*"

"*—one last question. Did he mention anything about a safe in his room?*"

A long beat.

Static.

Or a low wind

(conchlike).

"Ain' no mention of no safe, but he done gone n talk abou a locked door—reckon it needs a key or some kinda magic password" (a chuckle). "He goes on abou some kinda fish-number, claimin it's wha cracks thah door wiiiiiide open. Now, I tell yuh, I gah a soft spot for my Hector, but he sure gah a knack for speakin in riddles."

"What did he—"

"—time's up—"

"—say about this door?"

"Swore he'd never seh foot in them depths no more, n thah's precisely why he gone n done it. Says it's a clus'ered gatherin of macabre energies through thah fuckin door: an abysmal, metaphysical clus'erfuck of the highes' order, dark as the devil's asshole. Says it's the deepes' of deeps, the abyss's own abyss. His exact words, minus the profanity."

A beat. Chains clanking.

"One more question; do the numbers—"

"—time's up—"

"…3 2 1 mean anythi—"

End of file.

DEAR DR. SCHNEIDER,

I apologize for the apparent spontaneity of this correspondence, as we have not had the opportunity to interact previously. However, I find myself reaching out to you out of a sense of urgency, given your expertise in the field. I have been recommended your services by esteemed colleagues, such as Dr. Raelynn Combs and Dr. Randal Williamston, and have also come across your name during my own extensive research.

The reason I am seeking your assistance may appear multifaceted, but it is primarily centered around your areas of specialization. You see, you are not only renowned as a dream analyst but also one of the few psychologists/-iatrists who will openly discuss the effects of psychoactive substances like psilocybin and other psychedelics in the context of psychotherapy.

One of my patients has undergone an involuntary

encounter with psilocybin, where he was
unknowingly drugged by an individual. Perhaps you
recall hearing about this incident in the news; it
unfolded in a small coastal town called ██████████.
According to media reports — though I possess
additional information suggesting a far more sinister
and premeditated nature — he, ironically, endured
both a car accident and a mugging on the same night,
all the while being under the influence of the above-
mentioned psychedelic.

I mention this incident as a preamble to convey
the unusualness of the situation.

Following the incident, my patient engaged in a
single session of hypnosis, based on my suggestion...
which yielded <u>peculiar results</u>. Prior to the hypnosis
session, I had instructed my patient to maintain both
a dream journal and a regular journal simultaneously, as there had been perplexing instances of
overlap between the two, thus a catalyst for my
inquiring his willingness to be put under hypnosis.

Ever since the aforementioned event(s)
transpired (the psychedelic, the car accident, the
"mugging"), he has been "plagued by" — rather than
"suffering from," for he seems to receive a sense of
nirvana and even *meaning* (albeit *perceived*
meaning) of a higher order — peculiar nightmares
that seem intricately linked to the event(s) and,
more notably, the specific location where he
experienced the drug-induced state. There's also a

sense of déjà vu in these dreams which makes my client *believe* he's had them before.

This is where things get a bit metacontextual and esoterically subversive; for, as I describe to you the nature of his dreams, I feel it necessary to divide him into three distinct persons: the Dreamer (the temporal body of Felix Trellis; sleeping), the Passenger (his subconsciousness within the dream), and the Protagonist (which you'll understand shortly).

It goes something like this:

Almost invariably, the dream unfolds in or around the ocean. If the Dreamer finds his mind on a beach, he — whose dream-oriented subconsciousness I shall now refer to as the Passenger — ventures into the ocean. And if he is already submerged, he proceeds further until he reaches a chasm (or "void" or "abyss") at the bottom of the sea. At the precipice of this chasm, there always lies a tattered, ancient-looking book which he calls "The Swallowed Town." In the dream, on the ocean floor, near the chasm, the Passenger retrieves this book — or rather, manuscript — and begins reading from it. Curiously, it is penned by him (despite the antiquated nature of the book), or some version of him. I believe it represents a deeper iteration of his being, with all versions of himself aware of one another, except, perhaps, for the deepest incarnation — the Protagonist [of the manuscript].

The narrative within "The Swallowed Town" primarily develops in or around a darkhouse: the very location where the effects of the psilocybin first manifested for him. If you read my client's journal entries — both the "normal" ones and the dream entries — there's consistent mentioning of "nightfish," which he first saw during his *bad trip*. However, there are also notable mentions of certain key areas within this particular quasi-fictional locale: a downtown monument, a church, an academy, though the proximity to, or presence of, the darkhouse is most prevalent. Furthermore, he has occasionally alluded to — but sparingly referenced in his journal entries, often indirectly — that while reading from "The Swallowed Town" on the ocean floor, at the mouth of the chasm, within the dream, he perceives a discordant melody of "crab-clatter and waves and wind." Less frequently, but which alarms him with greater effect, my client reports that "something like formless, uninviting elevator music plays down there as I'm reading ['The Swallowed Town']; an almost forlorn wobble in the air/water, an antistatic so flat that it emblematically 'caves inward' or 'outward'; the audible wobbliness is like 'sandpaper'" (DreamJournal2.docx, starting at the fifth line down).

Attached to this email, you'll find a video file of our only hypnosis session so far, along with some scanned entries from his dream journals. I've also included a copy of what he scribbled on a piece of paper while under hypnosis, as seen in the footage. Please watch and view the scanned material before continuing. . . .

Do you believe what he wrote, under hypnosis, to be an indication of suicidal ideation? Words like "void," "oblivion," and "vacuous" — not to mention the overall mood from the text — seem like textbook red flags for progressively nihilistic outlooks, which could lead to self-harm. Also, do you believe that the Passenger exists as a buffer between the Protagonist and the Dreamer, to make his trauma more digestible? If so, it reminds me of a patient of mine from many years ago who, after his father's passing from cancer, had, via an acute anxiety-disorder episode, hallucinated a demonic crab; my working theory is that the disease was too mundane a thing to have killed his father, and so fabricating a demonic entity was the only way he knew how to compartmentalize the trauma. "The Swallowed Town" may be to my current patient as the cancer materializing as its astrological counterpart had been to my former patient. A buffering of trauma. There's something almost religious about it, too; parables seem to help the psyche absorb things too unpleasant or impalpable.

There is another reason I bring up my old patient. It has been years since I last saw him, but I still feel responsible for what I recently found out he had done: Cataloging his trauma for too long seemed to have become a band-aid rather than a cure, stretching his psyche past its threshold, which eventually led to an attempt to kill his stepfather. I have a similar worry for my current patient.

I'm sorry if this is a lot to take in under short notice, but I am genuinely worried he might do something reckless; and I'm ravenous to pick your brain on the matter.

An admirer,
Fatima Thawlen

The inviolate STRUCTURE

cyclopean

sleeping darkly
and always but never or sometimes
encroaching like an enigmatic
██████ made
of stone

and clay or BONE and
blood or the <u>residue</u>

of a god's GHOST <u>convergence</u>
of everythingness and
oblivion a beacon a <u>reliquary</u>

for not
only the vacuous emissaries or <u>THING</u>
the GREAT DOVE

GODS HAND

in the VOID but

the essence of <u>vacuity</u>
the soul of black itself

DAG ELOHIM

DEAR DR. THAWLEN,

Apologies for the delay in my response. I vaguely recall the incident you mentioned when it made headlines last year. It quickly turned into a contentious debate within my circles regarding psilocybin. I must emphasize the importance of a nuanced approach when dealing with hypnosis. What may hold true for Jack might not apply to Joe, let alone Jose. Factors such as age, gender, nationality, and religion form the foundational bedrock upon which experiences — like childhood or adulthood trauma — are layered. Perspective and worldview play a crucial role.

However, Dr. Thawlen, I will presume that you understand this and are applying it wisely. If I were to make an educated guess, I believe you are on the right track in deciphering his coping mechanism. After reviewing your attachments, it is my opinion that "The Swallowed Town" (as he calls it) does seem to act as a buffer between the bearable and the un-.

From what I gather, the only fatality in that incident
was another journalist named John R. Francis (along
with his would-be assailants). I would further deduce
that, though it remains speculative and cede that I
may be making deductions prematurely, this
traumatic reaction could stem from survivor's guilt.

But let me veer back to the topic of hypnosis.

The unconscious mind possesses an almost
supernaturally boundless nature that mankind
knows very little about. Moreover, what we currently
understand about it may be refuted in fifty years,
only to be replaced by entirely new findings a
century later. In many ways hypnosis, dreaming, and
psychedelics transport the individual to a similar
realm. However, it seems that hypnosis and
psychedelics are more advantageous (or detrimental,
which I'll explain momentarily) as forms of therapy.
It is akin to taming a wild horse. In dreams, your
subconscious resembles a mustang wandering
through an unfamiliar wilderness. The transition
between conscious and subconscious is so gradual
that the dreamer often remains unaware of the
dream state, and even if they do realize it,
attempting to fly or use superpowers becomes nearly
impossible without prior knowledge of the dream's
terrain.

In hypnosis, a saddle is placed upon that horse,
which is no longer a wild mustang but a domesticated
one. Actually it becomes a well-trained pony or

donkey. The hypnotized individual feels comfortable. The pony or donkey has traversed this path numerous times, even overcoming hilly and rugged terrain, ergo knowing the most efficient routes. Hypnosis serves as a valuable tool for teaching psychology, but most success stories, using it as a therapeutic method, are outliers. I often feel that hypnosis will eventually fade as a therapy relic and be relegated to a novelty for sideshow attractions. <u>It is too easy for the subject. The horse/pony/donkey is *too* well-trained. The subject does not have to exert effort, and there is no catharsis involved.</u>

Now, let us turn our attention to psilocybin. I understand that your email did not inquire about using it as a treatment method; rather it highlighted your patient's psychic experience with the psychedelic. However, it is important to understand that the hypnosis sessions may yield minimal results (if it had the potential of any at all) because psilocybin has already, figuratively speaking, beaten you to the punchline. Despite your patient having received the hallucinogen without consent or understanding, it has nonetheless acted as a form of psychotherapy à la self-hypnosis. Instead of a hypnotist employing the horse/pony/donkey with a saddle, <u>the patient is employing his own means of transportation.</u> In this case, a form of catharsis occurs (at least it has a more likely chance to). I hypothesize that that is why the effects have endured for such a prolonged period.

And I'll also hypothesize that it is not over yet, as your patient's "quest" remains incomplete.

I suggest exercising patience and observing your patient after the release of Hector Rowling. Will he continue to experience the multilayered dreams of the **darkhouse**, the abyss, and "The Swallowed Town," or will it fade? Keep a close watch and kindly provide me with an update sometime next month.

I hope this response addresses some of your queries.

If you have any further questions, insights, or observations, please do not hesitate to share them with me. Your dedication to understanding your patient's journey is commendable, and I am here to support you as best I can.

Warm regards,
Iain Schneider

r/theory Posted by u/GWIALP 3 days ago

HECTOR ROWLING AND THE LONG-REACHING MACHINATIONS OF THE FISH

I'M GOING TO SAY SOME nutty stuff (again), so just hear me out.

I'm not sure how many of you are following the Hector Rowling retrial—and if you are, is it for partisan political reasons (sorry, not sorry)? I'm not much interested in the question: "Should a person who is proven innocent"—if he actually IS innocent, because who knows if the evidence is even legit, and who knows if the jury/judge/whatever is objective)—"who prefers to be in prison, who in fact confessed to killing his family and who would (allegedly) do it again, should remain in prison?"

Listen, I get it. Prison is better than being homeless (assuming that the homelessness is from unfortunate life circumstances and having the social systems not work in their favor rather than from bad life decisions, like drug addiction—and in that case homelessness is almost always preferred; one time Russell Brand actually invited a homeless person to live with him with one stipulation that he had to take baths with him but the man chose to be homeless, or something like that, I don't know, but you get the point). Although, I also understand that prison is meant for the guilty—and it's not daycare, you know?

But the point of this post is something that (not so surprisingly due to our polarized, easily distracted, absent-of-critical-thinking times) most people aren't talking about:

IF Hector Rowling is innocent, and IF the court decides to toss out the evidence of his innocence in order to honor his preference for staying in prison, then the *actual* ax murderer will never be brought to justice.

Yes, sure, some of you are saying that the court may honor both—(1) keep Hector in prison, and (2) reopen the case and try to find the real killer...

...but I've got real problems with that. The chief problem is that that has never in the history of the United States—let alone the world—ever happened before. Never ever ever. More likely than not, the cops won't reopen that case, and their reason will simply be: Hector confessed.

And Hector *did* confess.

"But wait," those of you who regularly follow my posts may

be asking yourselves, "why are you so interested in this largely partisan debate, GretchenWhitmerIsALizardPerson? You're more into conspiracies and dark histories and all the macabre insanities that bump in the night, not politics. First of all, the western hemisphere of this planet has completely and utterly lost its mind, making everything under the sun a debate on morality or politics and global and social catastrophe, and a real-life version of *Watchmen*'s Ozymandias has yet to come up with a gigantic fake squid-alien invasion to amalgamate all of us again, to, as our country's name suggests, make us "united." THAT being said, you can't use the argument "you shouldn't talk about controversial/political topics" or "why are you being so political/controversial?"; it's not fair for people like me who just want to talk about things that are fascinating; everything finds its way to the mainstream because EVERYF***INGTHING is offensive or political nowadays. I'm not just going to stick my thumb in my mouth (or up my ass) and hope this social contagion of mass hysteria will just blow over. If I did, I'd be waiting for my turn to speak for decades and I'd eventually get bored enough to start to get curious what self-cannibalism would be like... and there would already a thumb in my mouth, so...

Second of all, for you faithful followers, there IS a conspiracy afoot.

I'm not actually all that surprised that nobody has looked into this. Because Hector Rowling's hometown is an anomaly of sorts.

It's a home to a cult, ladies and gents. I kid you not. And I think the only reason that it hasn't made it into the mainstream is because they haven't yet drunk the Kool-Aid like Jim Jones's followers. But just you wait. They will. One day. Also, they're not into witnessing to nonbelievers, nor do they have a charismatic leader recruiting susceptible, emotionally damaged individuals for him to secretly bang; they're pretty content on their cult/religion being a local thing.

So basically, hundreds of years ago three families get banned from their town for one of them practicing witchcraft (I'm not sure why they cast out THREE families instead of just ONE family [or one person] but I guess they wanted to be extremely thorough? Oh, those silly Puritans) and this caravan of hungry pilgrims finally make it to the coast of ▮▮▮▮▮▮ (Hector's hometown, although obviously this is *before* it was established). They're starving because the mean ol' Puritan town elders left them without any weapons (I mean, I guess if you're afraid one of them or all of them are witches or warlocks or wizards or some other w-word, you don't want to be like, "Hey ya'll, here's a bunch of weapons"—which makes me wonder if that's why witches and warlocks and wizards in fiction literature eventually just started walking around with, or waving, big sticks and little sticks [think about it]—just in case one of them or all of them are witches and warlocks and wizards and other w-words, and not the good kind either, no, but the post-temptation Saruman- or *Suspiria* types) and I guess they even tried to eat some plants but they kept on dying. I'm talking more than one person. Like a big fat handful of them. Almost like the land was cursed. (Or maaaaaaaybe one of them actually waaaaaaas a witch, wizard, warlock, or some other w-word, and was using black magic—for whatever nefarious reason—to harm the others; who knows!)

* cue dramatic *BUM BUM BUM* music. *

So yeah, they're pretty f***ing hungry, folks. And what happens—or at least what's *written* to have happened—is wacky. Oh, I probably should mention that this "cult" (or religion or lifestyle or belief-system or whatever-the-heck-you-want-to-call-it) predates Mormonism by almost two hundred years, so I'm sure some of it or all of it is exaggerated to some degree. And yes, one of the biggest theories is that out of desperation some of them or all of them ate [magic] mushrooms and tripped the f***k out. There are a few caveats which strawman that argument (I'll get to that later, if I remember to, but I'll probably forget—so hopefully you don't spend many nights tossing and turning in bed trying to think of what this one caveat may be; I apologize in advance), but I think people are mostly saying that because:

(a) the journalist who was responsible for proving Hector Rowling's innocence did in fact have psilocybin in his system when he survived that automobile accident last year WHILE investigating the Lighthouse Killings in ███████; and

(b) Joe Rogan says every religion is based on magic
mushrooms; but

I think it's low-hanging fruit, and there's no evidence to
suggest a mass-psychedelic experience. I'm not saying what
they claimed they saw (hold on, I'm getting to that) was
what actually happened, but I am saying that I think
something UNordinary DID happen. What that something is,
I don't know, but SOMETHING saved the community and is
why █████████ is the town that it is today.

Basically it went down like this: the outcasts were starving,
then after many days of their starving (in *The Second Book
of Jonah*, written by one of the pilgrim dudes named Charlie
Blackwood, who would become their "High Vicar" [I mean,
if that's not culty, I don't know what is, folks]), all of them—
not some, not most, *all*—saw a *thing* grab a whale or some
kind of big fish or shark from the ocean some distance from
the shoreline, lift it into the air, and, well... decimate it.
Crush it. Squish it. Squeeze it. (Choose your own verb) it.
One of the found-journals—from one of the town's
"founding parents," a man named Fredrick Grayson—states:

"... Angel—that of the Lord or of that of the Fallenness and
the Abyss of which is without the LORD GOD's grace, I know
not—squeezed to death one of our CREATOR's greatest fish of
the sea; its gore cascaded from the Heavens for nearly five
minutes, like a spattering thunderstorm volley; and my wife
said to me, 'Fredrick, this is the end of all things, the beast

from the sea, with seven heads and ten horns [and crowns] on its blasphemous heads,' but I, despite the outward darkness and seemingly palpable evil, squeezed her more tenderly than the angel squeezed the mighty sea-dwelling swine and said to her, 'Be not afraid.' Lo and behold, and after many hours of great trepidation, well beyond midnight, the flesh of that fish washed ashore. And its flesh was that of the manna for the Israelites in their arduous journey in the desert, and our fleshly, frail, mortal vessels were saved, destined to worship HIS glorious name."

Unlike the foundation of the Mormon faith, many many many many well-preserved journals (29, to be exact, very well safeguarded in a vault in the basement of The Museum of the Fish in █████████) back up this account—also, a good cover-story; a great way to undermine the cult-like qualities which the town has is to chalk it up as if all this sh** were collected just for history's sake. But I digress.

Pertaining to the predator which killed the whale/fish— some say "Great Dove," some say "Angel," some say "Archangel," some say "Daemon," one person said a "monstrously blasted manta ray," and the soon-to-be High Vicar himself said, "Literal Hand of God" (but gloved, because—"like GOD using the burning bush as bulwark between the finite and the infinite, between the fragility of man and the imperceivable nature of the LORD GOD, so too must HE wear a glove as not to annihilate our meat" *Second Book of Jonah* 1:12). Of course, some fringe scholars disagree on the meaning of the passage. Some believe

Blackwood implied that God/Yahweh/YHWH didn't want to "annihilate" the [whale/fish] meat, while others believe that Blackwood meant [not annihilating] the hungry pilgrims on the beach. Think what you want, but I think the latter makes more sense.

"But GWIALP," you may be asking, "why were all of these journal entries so meticulously and oh-so-conveniently preserved? It sounds like they're fabricated to me."

But I say, "nay nay," not fabricated per se; but calculated nonetheless, for certain. That's why I genuinely believe that SOMETHING HAPPENED. Oh hey, forgot to mention this, folks: Ol' Charlie Blackwood, the High Vicar—and this can be double- and triple- and quadruple-checked and verified by many, many of the journals—well, he was pretty much a Richard Dawkins/Christopher Eric Hitchens/Bill Maher-caliber of Atheist. I'm talking literally up to the moment prior to the event (by all means, his marrying the woman who got them banished from their town is evidence enough; that's right, he married, like, a legit witch named Alma Rowling [she even kept her last name after their being married, which in the 1600s is pretty much unheard of; blasphemous even]. I guess she even cut off a dog's head, burnt its tongue [as an offering? An offering to WHAT? who knows], and put roses in its—you guessed it—"hollowed-out eyes" [six different journals verify this]). Since the journals are dated, we know that he fell head over heels for God at least five days after the aforementioned event happened. It's because Charlie Blackwood had such strong convictions about what occurred that he put in the effort to preserve the documents. I mean, listen: this isn't new to religious phenomena. It's one of the reasons why the Old Religions have survived. And as you guys who have been following me—the Mulder of Forums and Blogs—know: this is where I harshly deviate from the sort of "modern idea" that all religions are forms of "patriarchal manipulation in order to oppress," for I truly truly TRULY believe that the progenitors of all the Old Religions—and I'm talking the ancient scribes who penned the substratum of Judeo-Christianity (i.e., the Tanakh/Old Testament), were True Believers—as was Charlie Blackwood—but that's not to say there haven't been political, Trumpian manipulators of such creeds throughout history.

(Heck, if I saw what I thought was "God's literal hand" reaching into the ocean and squeezing a big fat whale and having—what I believe, anyway—its flesh wash ashore and save my friends and family from starvation, I'd probably sign up to be one of the Church of the Fish's deacons myself [i.e., "the School of Yahweh"]; especially considering of how antireligious/antisocial/antieverything Charlie Blackwood was prior to the event.)

So—now a True Believer in more of the OT, more-or-less Judaic God than the NT God (hence my usage of Yahweh or, the more accurate "word," YHWH)—Charlie Blackwood constructed the church and built a lighthouse too (not sure why)—

—pump the brakes, folks—

—did you guys know that Hector Rowling lived in Charlie Blackwood's lighthouse? Hector's father was a lighthouse keeper, and Hector—since he was the oldest, actually *only*, son (family traditions and all that jazz)—was set to be the lighthouse keeper himself when his father retired or died. Died? Well, hey, his father *did* die. Or did he? The police found literal gallons of his blood in the lantern room (top of the lighthouse, in case you didn't know), which they assumed belonged to Mr. Rowling... but there was no body. Weird, huh? I mean, really. Really weird. Really REALLY weird because it suggests a few things:

Firstly, it would suggest that Hector killed his father first; he had to have, right? But where did the body go? Wouldn't his mom and sister have seen him moving body parts? And if his father wasn't first, then he must have been so enthralled with his work in the lantern room that he didn't hear his son killing the entire family with a hatchet downstairs (plus, Hector's sister was under her bed and probably screaming bloody murder—how would Daddy not have heard her?).

Secondly, where did the body parts go? How did Hector move them before the cops arrived?

Thirdly, apparently the blood in the lantern room was black as oil and moldering with fruiting bodies.

Of course the alternative theory is that he did kill his father first. Went downstairs and killed his sister and mother. Went back upstairs and did what he did with his father's body (even though there was hardly any blood on him, which is one of the main reasons why the evidence so strongly suggests his innocence).

The truth is... you can pick holes in this all day long. It's an impossible game of Jenga; it's always going to be lopsided and awkward and on the verge of collapse; a rigged game. The only thing that truly makes sense—*practically,* anyway—is for there to have been more than one killer. One of them took care of Daddy in the lantern room, another went after the sister in the bedroom, then took care of the mother somewhere in the living room; or maybe there was a third one who took care of the mother, and maybe Hector just happened to be gone for the day and came home to a bloody f***ing massacre and the killers scrammed and he took the blame. Apparently, the killers' impetus—according to journalist Felix Trellis, the state of ▮▮▮▮▮▮▮, and many people on Twitter—was to break into a safe in Hector's room. It would pretty much be the plot of *In Cold Blood* had the son not been on the spectrum so as to allow the cops to convince him that he was the killer and so he confessed and then, because of his pretty apparent autism (I'm not saying that hyperbolically, of course, and it shouldn't be offensive because the State's lawyers are using that angle), he sort of became accustomed to prison and therefore he didn't/still doesn't want to leave (and blah blah blah). That's the mainstream narrative, and hey, it makes sense.

But I don't think that's right. And no, I'm not siding with the rightwing-ish viewpoint that "just because he's on the spectrum doesn't mean he's not guilty or accountable" or that "if he is innocent, then he shouldn't be imprisoned even if he wants to stay." While I do understand those POVs, I think that's wrong. Or maybe *almost* right—but for the wrong reasons.

Because it's missing something: something profoundly vital. You know, there's a golden rule in journalism: *follow the money*. That's *usually* the case. And it would be the case here, too, if there was any money in that safe. But what I ask to you, GWIALP followers, is... what transcends money?

Creed.

Faith.

Religion.

The Fish.

I'm talking about conviction from True Believers, like how Susan Atkins, Linda Kasabian, Patricia Krenwinkel, and "Tex" killed for Manson; they were crazy, sure, but they were crazy for Manson, crazy for something greater, for something beyond the material world, beyond the mundanity of this— as Rustin Cohle from *True Detective* says—"giant gutter in outer space." I think it's all too convenient that Hector's great ancestor was the founder of the Church of the Fish, built the lighthouse that he and his family lived in; too convenient that a shut-in like Brian Maxwell had the social capacity to call, email, even text John R. Francis (RIP) and Felix Trellis; too convenient that a sixty-year-old Native American war vet who volunteered at the local Museum would be one of the murderers just because he had some gambling debt (pretty weak motive, imo); too convenient that the cult angle isn't even mentioned, neither by the plaintiff (the town of ███████████) nor defendant (state of ████████) nor FBI.

I know this is a half-formed theory, but I just want to give you all some food for thought.

TL;DR: It looks like there might an occult element to this whole Hector Rowling situation.

For more detailed info, please check out Ron Ullman's *A Dark History of the Families of the Fish* (his grandson, who also writes books, was recently on a pretty interesting podcast called *Gorgon Mania*—rumor has it that he's related to Hector's mother Rita, and has some inside, intimate, macabre details on the town and its religion).

Also, don't forget to check out my blog—it's called Gretchen Whitmer Is A Lizard Person—where you can find other essays (the "Elkhourne Horror" one you can't actually Google search [I wonder why *cough, cough, COUGH!!!*], so you actually have to go to my blog), such as:

THE DARK SECRET OF THE ELKHOURNE HORROR IN COYOTE VILLAGE, MI

THE MYSTERIOUS GINGER OF THE APOCALYPSE

AMERICAN MISSIONARIES GO TO BRAZIL AND ALMOST END THE WORLD

HAMPTON, PA, OUTBREAK COVER-UP

and

ELISA LAM WAS SACRIFICED BY BASATAN CULTISTS

AdamFellagain2Hell 3d ago
Way to self-rpormoste.

AdamFellagain2Hell 3d ago
Promote*

> **TheTruthIsOutThair1989 ADMIN** 3d ago
> You literally just joined two weeks ago; if you were a
> regular to this forum then you would know that Big
> Papa GWIALP has a little bit more freedom to do
> what he wants regarding self-promo. (Also, stop
> promoting your amateurish self-published
> CreepyPasta short stories here, and stop making fake
> profiles to upvote. Thank you ☺)

> > **AdamFellagain2Hell** 3d ago
> > You're probably GWIALP, that's why you allow
> > him/you to promote hisself/yourself and not

other people.

> **TheTruthIsOuTtHAIR1989** ADMIN 3d ago
> I could only wish I was Big Papa GWIALP.

KellyGunMachineBoy 3d ago
am i the only 1 who thinks this title sounds like a harry potter book if u replaced hector rowling with harry potter or is it just me

JCRoadWarrior 2d ago
Wait a minute, GWIALP. I think I've got another piece of the puzzle. I'm surprised you hadn't mentioned it.

> **CarkosaSurfer14** 2d ago
> ?

KamehamehaGod 2d ago
Care to elaborate or do you just want to get GWIALP's attention?

> **JCRoadWarrior** 2d ago
> No, I just thought maybe he forgot this part. Or that he actually believed the—I guess you could say 'urban legend,' and didn't want to say it for that reason.

> > **CarkosaSurfer14** 1d ago
> > ????

DahnJoe 1d ago
You're talking about BVT?

TheTruthIsOutThair1989 ADMIN 1d ago
/u/AdamFellagain2Hell, is this one of your fake
profiles and another CreepyPasta reject concept?

AdamFellagain2Hell 1d ago
[comment deleted]

GWIALP 1d ago
Actually **/u/TheTruthIsOutTheir1989**,
/u/JCRoadWarror isn't wrong—well, wrong about
my accidentally forgetting to mention it, but not
wrong about what **/u/DahnJoe** mentioned. BVT—
or "black van theory," has been circulating for
quite some time. But at the moment I don't know
how to extract fact from fiction with BVT. Even on
the Gorgon Mania podcast, Ron "Wayward"
Ullman mentions seeing this black van when he
looked out his window as a kid—prior to finding
his grandparents brutally murdered (yeah, I guess
that opens up another can of worms too, but this
took place in Michigan): *"a big black shark
or... something. Lying still. Very, very still. On my
driveway. Big dull eyes staring at me. Challenging
me. Then it swims away, wraithlike, down our long
and windy driveway, through the trees, to the
road, and it vanishes"* There's an idea that this
was not a literal shark (duh), but a car of some

sort. And Felix Trellis claims to also have been "chased" by a black van. However, it should be mentioned that no vehicle was found at the beach. Personally, I think that the bodies were placed there and weren't actually the original perpetrators; or at the very least there was a getaway driver; or everything's a coverup.

> **JCRoadWarrior** 19h ago
>
> Don't forget the released audio of John R. Francis's interview with what's-his-face. He wanted John to walk around his house, looking out windows, going upstairs not to just look out the windows but to make sure the windows were closed and locked. Very peculiar. And what was that scream? No closure has ever come from that.

AdamFellagain2Hell 19h ago

[comment deleted]

AdamFellagain2Hell 19h ago

[comment deleted]

AdamFellagain2Hell 18h ago

Very mature, **/u/TheTruthIsOutThair1989**.

GWIALP_BACKUP_ACCT 40m ago

[comment deleted]

GWIALP 39m ago

On second thought, in light of the news of Hector Rowling's arrival back at ██████, everything I said was wrong. He is innocent, he shouldn't be in prison even if he wanted to be, he deserves to be home.

KamehamehaGod 30m ago

That doesn't sound like you. Blink if someone's holding a gun to your head.

EsotericaPhilosophy 1d ago

Piggybacking off of your True Believer idea, and also going BEYOND it, what would be the logical *origo cogitationis* of this "cult"? Why put the fish that swallowed Jonah on such a high pedestal in the same way Catholicism does Mary? Rhetorical question(s) because I have an idea or two after reading up on the creed of ██████. There are a few things to unpack first.

Firstly, what is the abyss? Literally, what is it? It comes from the Greek word "abyssos"; it means bottomless/unfathomable—a primeval, chaotic void. You could say the unknown; as Friedrich Nietzsche famously wrote, ". . . if you gaze long enough into an abyss, the abyss will gaze back into you." But I also think it is—if not synonymous with, then certainly related to—"death," the final frontier. But there's also—at least in modern thinking—an oceanic association to the abyss, too, but I think The Church of the Fish somehow has combined the concepts with the Fish and the Great Dove.

But to further illustrate this "death" analogy: They were literally almost dead when the Great Dove fed them flesh from the Fish. They were at death's/the abyss's door. Figuratively and literately and, in some ways, metaphysically and metaliterally.

In Charlie Blackwood's *Second Book of Jonah*, 12:24, he writes a slightly modified version of Genesis 1:2 ("Now the earth was formless and empty, darkness was over the surface of the deep, and the Spirit of God was hovering over the waters").

What he writes is this: "The Abyss, shapeless and vacant, lay shimmering under the Hand of God." Of course he takes this in a radically apocryphal direction when he goes on to say in *SBOJ* 14:3 that "the Abyss is [God's] Firstborn child, and Its children dwelt under the surface of the deep," and in 15:5, he even says that the Great Flood was a pact between [God] and "His Firstborn" to "appease its voracious appetite; so must we do the same?" I will mention that there is a debate on whether this is meant to be a period or a question mark—the original document is slightly smudged. Those who argue for the "?" claim that it's meant as a rhetorical question of sorts, that the obvious answer is "no," because that would be wicked. But skeptics of Charlie Blackwood and his church/cult believe that he actually thinks his followers should, I don't know, sacrifice people? There's a lot of speculation among the locals and historians.

Okay, I know I'm kind of . . . I guess . . . coming at this from a few different angles. Might seem like I'm aimless. But I wanted to set up the Abyss-centeredness of that whole subset of Judaism for a particular reason. And this is also coming from someone who likes to come at supernaturalism in a grounded way but also one that doesn't lose its supernaturalism. This is also coming from a Christian—and no, I'm not being preachy; I'm a conspiracy theorist like you guys, but I also like to apply what I believe may be true. But even if the religious/divine aspects aren't true, maybe the scribes of these books misunderstood—but that doesn't necessarily mean that they're not supernatural..

I'm going to write a few passages from the Bible and enclose key words or passages in Asterisks.

Revelation 21:8— . . . they will be consigned to a *fiery lake* of burning sulfur.

Psalms 9:17— The wicked go down to the *realm of the dead*, all the nations that forget God.

2 Thessalonians 1:9— They will be punished with everlasting destruction and *shut out from the presence of the Lord* . . .

A "fiery lake" may be an ocean; "realm of the dead" may

be the ocean after the Great Flood; "shut out of presence of the Lord" may be literally the absence of God or light, aka the Abyss.

To be honest, I forgot the point I was trying to make. It's kind of like that Tenacious D song, "Tribute," in which the song was only a tribute to the greatest song in the world; and I suppose this is only a tribute to a better theory I had a few days ago but now I can't catch all my little strands of thought. I guess my point is: what if the founders of the Church of the Fish witnessed a fallen angel, something truly evil, and mistook it for something good. And what if the ocean is Hell? I mean, it's a really big place, and what if the water is just a third-dimensional veil of sorts?

GWIALP 1d ago

As you know, I'm not against there being truth in myth. You bring up some interesting points—points that I hadn't thought about. And to be fair, some of the excommunicated pilgrims did think the thing from the sea may have been of demonic origin. However, I have a hard time wrapping my head around why a demon/fallen angel would have wanted to feed them.

EsotericaPhilosophy 1d ago

It would have wanted what ALL the fallen angels would have wanted: to be treated like a god. To be worshiped.

GWIALP 1d ago

Hmmm… interesting approach. I dig it.

KellyGunMachineBoy 1d ago

aliens bro. i mean theres no way the entire earth flooded unless the water was from another planet you know? i mean thats "piggybacking" off of your taking bible stories seriously and whatnot but also putting a supernatural spin on it. maybe all the salt water on earth today was originally from planet x. but im not as smurt as the rest of ya'll.

GWIALP 1d ago

Lmao. That's actually an innovative idea. You two are getting my theory-gears turning.

JCRoadWarrior 18h ago

That's an interesting theory on the worldwide flood. Firstly, you're right. There isn't enough water in the sky (via clouds) to flood the earth. So it would be impossible. At least today it would be. HOWEVER, if there was enough water in the sky to flood the earth, there would have to be a TON OF IT. Now, what would that look like? Well, there would be a "Green House Effect" of sorts; the water would cause a quasi-prism effect, heat bouncing back and forth. The entire earth would have been tropical—and we do have scientific evidence to support this.

This theory also plays to the fact that the rainbow was God's sign that he wouldn't flood the earth again. If taken literally (not figuratively, not religiously metaphorical), this would mean that the first time it ever rained on earth it flooded completely (there's an interrelation regarding an asteroid being the catalyst for the first and very cataclysmic rainfall—that's only if a worldwide flood happened naturally but mankind put a supernatural twist on it). This would also explain how in the north they found a mammoth completely preserved and eating food; insinuating that one second it was minding its own business, grazing the pastures, and then the next second, when the waters started falling, the "Green House Effect" nullified immediately and it turned into a mammoth ice cube.

Another argument relates to fossils. For instance, an archeologist found this one crab with a scuttle-trail observable (it obviously wasn't alive for millions or billions of years— sediment had quite suddenly covered it and pressed it down, but it still managed to move a couple feet before becoming fossilized). Also there are fossilized trees that are standing upright—what happens when trees die? They fall over. They don't stand upright for billions of years allowing dirt to gradually fossilize around their bases. So again, for a tree to remain standing, it appears—logically and scientifically—to have been covered with sediment and fossilized very, very quickly. Two other notes on fossils: (1) several years back, a modern clock had been found fossilized (I think in New York, but I may be wrong) with an estimated age of a few million years; and (2) in labs they're able to completely fossilize material within a short span of time—they concluded it has more to do with PRESSURE (like tons and tons and tons of water) and less to do with immeasurable amounts of TIME.

Of course there's no "extraordinary evidence" regarding this; but there are lots and lots of ancient civilizations that have stories of a worldwide flood. Now, did they all get together at Stonehenge and corroborate on a basic outline for this legend; or was it like a game of telephone?—it happened, and over time the details changed as it passed through each ancient civilization?

Shrug.

According to this theory—because of how

apocalyptically, cosmically overwhelming the rainfall would have had to have been (not to mention Genesis 7:11 regarding not just the deep springs but the *great* deep springs bursting open)—this cataclysm could have also facilitated the splitting of Pangaea; the argument is that this would have been so devastating that it may have taken anywhere from decades (or less) to a hundred years for the continents to stabilize rather than millions or billions of years.

I'll also say that as an atheist, this is interesting because even Graham Hancock and Randall Carlson believe they've found evidence of a "recent" worldwide flood. Of course I'm getting all of this from the Joe Rogan podcast; I haven't read their book or anything.

To bring it full circle, in the context of **/u/EsotericaPhilosophy**'s original comment, there is some secular science to back up a "more recent worldwide flood."

PS. Maybe the asteroid that caused the flood had alien lifeforms on it. Food for thought.

AdamFellagain2Hell 10h ago

[comment deleted]

TheTruthIsOutThair1989 ADMIN 9h ago

Hey dude, this forum is like Planet Fitness. Judgment free. We are inclusive to all creeds, races, genders, ages, politics, cultures, nationalities—you name it. How can we scratch the surface of a Greater Truth if we can't explore ALL possibilities? Please don't call anybody—or anybody's theory—stupid. And if you were to pay attention to the context of what was said by **/u/JCRoadWarrior**, you would have realized they didn't actually believe it (or at least never explicitly said so); they were only stating a theory.

This is your last warning. We want enlightenment, not trolls.

LBarronStoleMyMum 17h ago

You guys heard the news, right? About what happened to Hector Rowling? He was released today -- or was supposed to be. The news is being hush-hush. And you know what, guys? You know how when you get out of prison and usually you have someone waiting for you to pick you up (not saying you-you, Im just saying "you" in a general sense), although I suppose sometimes recently freed inmates -- ex-inmates, technically -- take a prison-offered bus. Ive seen that happen in movies, so I dunno if thats real. AAANNNYYWAY!!! Point being. My friends brother works at that prison, which is why I just made this account literally two minutes ago because Ive heard GWIALP on some podcast with Alex Jones a while back and I know he/you/whoever who is on this forum would be interested in this detail. Anyway, my friends brother says a black van was there to pick him up. Apparently the plan was that a bus was going to drop him off in the city, you know, cuz I guess the bus was there, too. But he saw the van.

My friends brother says that Hector got really really white but at the time he didnt think anything of it. Just a black van, right? --Might not even have been for him, says my friends brother, --but there was a look of pure dread, as if he saw something that wasnt there. That the black van was something else to him. Like a ghost. But my friends brother also says Hector was a little on the eccentric or maybe autistic side, so he didn't think anything of it (at the time).

Hector didnt move. Said something like, --I want to go back. Kept repeating it. --I want to go back I want to go back I want to go.

--But dude youre free.

--Go back go back go back back back back!

Yeah he went full Hodor, I guess. But unlike Hodor who made it a mission statement in his life, Hector Rowling went outside -- my friends brother thought he was going to the bus -- then he took a sharp left turn, disappeared around the side of the prison. I mean, they didnt exactly chase after him -- he was a free man. Though they were confused. Then --the black van, says my friends brother, --just sort of ... casually drifted away. But get this. Said it drove so smoothly it might have been in water.

> **AdamFellagain2Hell** 17h ago
>
> [comment deleted]

> **AdamFellagain2Hell** 17h ago
>
> [comment deleted]

JonahTheTrueDisciple_23921 17h ago

The Apostate was weakened by that human-verminity; turned his brain to mush; he took the easy way out instead of taking responsibility and giving himself wholly to the Great Formless Brine Beyond, but - fear not - he is reborn anew nonetheless. An incarnation of Father Shachor.

> **KellyGunMachineBoy** 16h ago
>
> whut r u on bro

> **TheTruthIsOutThair1989** ADMIN 16h ago
>
> This is so off topic but also weirdly entertaining enough to allow it.

JonahTheTrueDisciple_23921 14h ago

Dag Elohim.

Will you kindly stop discussing things about which you have little to no understanding? All of you are like

invasive mildew, oxidizing your way toward the Great
Formless Brine Beyond . . .

. . . as the Suffering Witch sang as she burnt in the Sea:

". . . As if a corpse rejoices in festivity,
Within the theater macabre, their thoughts persist,

"Chains of axioms shattered, they ascend,
Beyond the mortal guise, their true form revealed,
An allegiance forged amidst the abyss's abyss . . ."

EsotericaPhilosophy   14h ago
Quoting from The Second Book of Jonah 32:4.
Somebody did their homework.

GWIALP_BACKUP_ACCT   39m ago
[comment deleted]

GWIALP_BACKUP_ACCT   39m ago
[comment deleted]

LBarronStoleMyMum   1h ago
Update:

This hasnt made the news yet but Hector Rowling
jumped off an overpass. He landed atop a moving
eighteen-wheeler, rolled off, landed on the freeway, then
got ran over by another eighteen-wheeler. Looks like he
really did not want to leave prison.

But the weird thing is: his body was taken. Some people are saying that a black van pulled up beside him and scooped him up, guts and all.

JCRoadWarrior 40m ago

So the plot thickens, eh? **/u/GWIALP**, what say you?

GWIALP 40m ago

Sounds farfetched. People found him at church in ██████████.

Let's just move on from this. There are better things to talk about.

GWIALP_BACKUP_ACCT 39m ago

[comment deleted]

GWIALP_BACKUP_ACCT 38m ago

[comment deleted]

GWIALP_BACKUP_ACCT 38 ago

[comment deleted]

GWIALP_BACKUP_ACCT 37 ago

[comment deleted]

JonahTheTrueDisciple_23921 25m ago

We all must return to Dag Elohim, YHWH's firstborn child.

KellyGunMachineBoy 21m ago

lol i see whut ur doing nice very funny

KamehamehaGod 16m ago

Someone posted a vid on TikTok of the accident—well, it was about thirty seconds after he jumped—and it looks like black ooze instead of blood. But yeah. There's no direct evidence that it was Hector Rowling. He wasn't wearing the same clothes he left prison in, but he might have quickly changed—if of course he was hiding/running from someone/some persons—but get this:

The TikTok reel showed a black van stopping and people in black getting out. They were wearing hoods, had masks on. The footage is obviously really blurry, because of course it is.

Seems like they may have been wearing gasmasks.

    JCRoadWarrior 13m ago

    So the plot thickens—again.

GWIALP 10m ago

Hey everyone, someone anonymously Skyped me a live feed of a lighthouse a few hours ago. I took a screenshot and then Googled the ▮▮▮▮▮▮ lighthouse. Same one. Then my webcam, er, randomly turned on—you all should know that I always keep black tape over it, so I'm good.

Or… I thought I was good. Then I suddenly got logged off. I didn't immediately think it was suspicious because sometimes (at least I suspect) my girlfriend signs onto my account from her phone to make sure I am not "talking to any T.H.O.T.s" (I'm sure you fellas know what I'm talking about). But that wasn't the case, since I realized that my girlfriend had left her phone in my office. And she also keeps her one and only laptop in my office, too. I even went upstairs and found her watching *Vampire Diaries* for, like, the millionth time.

I tried to sign back on. I couldn't.

Then I signed on to my backup account and saw that my main account had posted a few things. Everyone, listen up, I'm not pranking you in order to validate my theory. This sh*t happened. I did not say this:

"Sounds farfetched. People found him at church in 
.
Let's just move on from this. There are better things to talk about."

Then my backup account got deleted. Almost immediately. I'm going to try to bring it back but if you ever see a new username called "GWIALP_BACKUP_ACC2," then it's me.

Maybe this is just a prank. Maybe

/u/AdamFellagain2Hell is mad at some of us for instigating (if so, I'm sorry—I personally enjoy all of your CreepyPasta-esque theories; if not, I'm creeped out because we might have the equivalent of a pyromaniac watching his work burn and bating his fiery desires with his masterful hand: in other words, folks, this may inadvertently prove my theory).

AdamFellagain2Hell 9m ago

That wasn't me. I can barely wipe my own butt let alone hack into your account. But I am sorry for being petty about the self-promo comment, I guess I was tired of either getting downvoted or completely ignored, I'm not sure if the algorithm hates me or if everyone else does. And I appreciate the compliment.

KellyGunMachineBoy 8m ago

id like to go on record to say that I can wipe my butt, but it wasn't me either

JCRoadWarrior 7m ago

Black tape is up. Locking doors tonight. Keeping an eye out for a black friggin van too.

GWIALP_BACKUP_ACC2 1m

You will all be swallowed by Dag Elohim.

FELIX'S JOURNAL (FINAL ENTRY)

IF YOU'RE READING THIS, then that means a hyperreality that hums below the surface of the deceptively thin veil of all things has engulfed me; if you're reading this, then I am with Brian Maxwell (the real one), John R. Francis, and all the nameless others; if you're reading this, then I have come to

(THE SWALLOWED TOWN)
█████████ as a tourist of the Festival of the Fish—a passerby, a voyeur, an acolyte, a scuttling crab with its shell oozing death, and reeking; if you're read this, then I am Ishmael.

I TOLD MYSELF I WOULDN'T surrender to the news vortex—alas, resistance proved futile. It became my narcotic fix, an addiction pulsating through my veins, insatiable hunger gnawing at my journalistic aspirations, and my equally insatiable curiosity regarding the enigma known as Hector Rowling—though I mostly steered clear of the seething political battleground regarding his right to remain in prison as a 'resident of choice' (whatever that means).

And so it happened: receiving the news that he had flung himself from the overpass—a dance with death that culminated in a semi-truck running him over—had formed in my life (once been a picturesque, rustic town nestled by the sea) a churning, ravenous abyss. And the ruthless torrents and crashing waves of calls and text messages and emails and unanswered knocks at my apartment door: a cacophony of clamoring voices eager to "check up" on me or solicit a quote for a motley assortment of magazines, journals, and grotesquely corrupted news outlets.

Dr. Thawlen called the police to do a wellness check on me.

Two cops materialized. I, a hapless puppet, obeyed their rapping knuckles by opening the door. To them I must have appeared feral: a man with an uncultivated mane, a dark complexion juxtaposed against a soiled garment, and eyes bloodshot and vacant. It even occurred to me, as I looked at the two men—trained hands resting on their service pistols—that with their lizard brains they may have painted the disheveled canvas before them with an alternative narrative due to my *blackness*. And I suddenly felt self-conscious and fearful that they may have misconstrued the dry-erase marker in my hand as a knife.

Cop 1: *We're just checking up on you, Mr. Trellis. Is everything all right?*

They of course recognized me—I'd made national news. Twice. I may not have been a traditional celebrity, but I was certainly coasting off a rather prolonged fifteen minutes of fame.[20]

---

[20] I was also insulted that they had so easily recognized me rather than mistake me for an intruder, since I more closely resembled one than the man or journalist or dreamer known—or

Cop 2, after giving Cop 1 a sideways glance: *Crappy hand you were dealt. Sorry about the Rowling thing. Prison can mess people up real bad. Recidivism—or in this case, Stockholm Syndrome. We'll be leaving, Mr. Trellis, but do us a favor and call your therapist.*

Cop 1: *Are you gonna write a novel about this stuff?*

I almost said: *I'm not that kind of writer.* But I cut off my tongue (metaphorically, obviously) just before speaking because I didn't know any longer *which* version of myself I was—Journalist-Felix or *Swallowed Town*-Felix or a deeper, more lost variant of Felix.

I can't remember what I instead told them. It must've been satisfactory enough because of the way they glanced at one another. The smaller and older of the two nodded, sighed, and wiped the sweat from his brow like he'd just disabled a ticking time bomb.[21]

---

maybe, at this point, even *formerly known*—as Felix Trellis.

[21] Who knows, maybe he had . . . at least, at the time, I thought he had; but, since you're reading this, I think we both know that he hadn't disabled the bomb, and it ticked and it ticked and it tock tock tocked and here I am going over my earlier journal entries and adding footnotes for you at this shoddy motel where next door kids are screaming and seagulls in the parking lot are screaming and the ocean wind pressing against the walls and windows, clawing its way under the door—a low wind

(*conchlike*)

ON TWITTER, someone (a ███████ local) claimed to have spotted Hector Rowling at the Church of the Fish. This got my hopes up even though I knew the trolls and conspiracy theorists had infiltrated the conversation by that point, claiming Rowling had never left prison and instead ~~a lookalike left in his place~~.

Scratch that. Someone else chimed in—"from a *valid* source, so this is a hundred percent true and definitely NOT A QAnon CONSPIRACY!!!!"—insisting the prison had released a clone, programmed to run as if he were guilty and throw himself off an overpass, "because the government doesn't want people constantly getting out of prison"

(*so why did they need to clone him?* asked @rumPtor23

isn't it obvious? isn't the answer so easy to see? @AdamFellagain2Hell

*if it's easy then it's easy to explain why the f***ing government would clone and program him to jump off a bridge!* @rumPtor23

it's an overpass, you dumbass, Troll 1

I heard he and Jeffrey Epstein are both CIA inform-ants and you're right @rumPtor23, he was a clone be-cause Trump is building an army of people with special abilities to overtake the liberal government—they're gon-na arrest Obama, Biden, Clinton [both of them], Bill Gates, Bill Nye the Science Guy, The Young Turks, and Don Lemon, Troll 2).

TWO INTERNET SLEUTHS—a married couple who pro-

—is screaming.

duced true-crime content on YouTube and TikTok—had found a similar black van with tinted windows and plates. They followed it for a while but lost the trail when they stopped to refuel.

Had it been the same van as the one that had followed me? Same make? I wasn't sure except for the color.

Black.

An unnamed pedestrian had then found said van smoldering in a wreckage on Interstate ██. The police and the news were hush-hush for a couple of days, and even during a small press conference a few days later there was no mention of Hector Rowling. The speaker— an overweight Native American man whose pockmarked face glistened from heat- and nerve-induced sweat and the ruthlessly blasting Cajun sun—said (and in a moment it became clear why they had a measly captain speaking rather than a major, lieutenant colonel, or the big cheese himself—which also had something to do with the man's overt nervousness), occasionally dabbing his face with a handkerchief:

"Thank you, everyone, for your patience. A few days ago a van was found on the side of Interstate ██. *Burning."*

The microphone made his voice sound robotic, and the camera broadcasting the conference (I was watching it on YouTube on my iPhone) made him look gray. He coughed and looked around. There were camera flashes.

"Debris scattered across the freeway—also burning. One of the reasons why it's taken so long for us to relay information to the public was because of the conditions the deceased were in"—slight commotion from the press, a hand raised and appropriately ignored—*"conditions which rendered conventional identifying methods futile. None of the four people, neither their dental nor their*

fingerprints—for the ones whose fingerprints we were able to use, that is—were found in the system. Forensics was, however, able to identify sex; all were male. And ethnicity; all were Native American—"

The press pressed for an answer via whirlwind of incoherent babble.

"The deceased were found wearing black raincoats and black rainboots. They had on their hands black rubber gardening gloves. They used duct tape, also black, to seal where their gloves and raincoat sleeves connected."

He turned and glanced at one of the Big Cheeses, then turned toward the press and cleared his throat before saying:

"We'd like to make this next point crystal clear: there is no indication—as some corners of the internet have been suggesting—that there was anything criminal, at least from a forensics' perspective, about the wreckage. Thank you, and I'll take a few questions."

Reporter 1: *"Is there any indication that this was a racially motivated attack?"*

The captain—for this certainly was the reason for which his superiors had chosen him to be the talking head on this matter—coolly responded, *"It was a motor vehicle collision. Next."*

Reporter 2: *"A recent viral video shows people, all wearing gas masks, getting out of what seems to be the same black van."* Reporter 2 failed to mention the most vital part—how they scooped up Hector Rowling like roadkill—and I almost whipped my phone across the room because of it. *"Can you confirm if the van found in the wreckage is the same from the video?"*

Another glance to his superiors.

"The forensics report did not suggest that."

Reporter 2: *"Is it possible that the gas masks from*

the video could have been burnt in the fire?"

A shrug. *"That's in the realm of guesswork, and I'm not forensics—next."*

Reporter 3: *"Other drivers on the road witnessed a tall column of white light appearing just before the car somersaulted off the highway. There's speculation as to it being an airstrike. Any comments?"*

The captain bugged out his eyes (resulting in a gaggle of whispers via indecipherability of his expression), glanced over his shoulder at a black man in a suit and tie whose aura sang "professorial" rather than "law enforcement," and then turned back toward Reporter 3, and said slowly, with the same buggy eyes, *"Motor. Vehicle. Collision. Not . . . whatever you're suggesting."* He shrugged and shook his head. *"Let's have one more question. Yes?"*

Reporter 4: *"Hi there. A Mr. and Mrs. McKenzie— farmers who live on the property just off Interstate ▮▮— have made multiple complaints to the police with no definitive answer; so I feel like it's my obligation to speak on their behalf—"*

The captain: *"What were their complaints about?"*

"A black substance—found growing off the interstate. Origin seems to be the wreckage site. They claim its spreading onto their property."

"I don't hear a question, ma'am."

"Do the police know what that substance is?"

The *professorial* black man pressed a finger to his ear and exited the frame. I turned up my phone's volume and listened to the captain talk—*"again, I cannot speak to anything which wasn't listed in the forensics report"*— before going to the bathroom of my little apartment and looking into the trashcan where I'd been actively ignoring that which stared back—[22]

Lightheadedness came over me as the phone muffledly buzzed near the faucet.

I found myself back at ▮▮▮▮▮▮▮ Hospital.

A black man—not the *professorial* one from the press conference, but another one—was sitting next to me as I lay on the hospital bed.

The man said something.

His lips moved, no words came out, had a wheelchair, said something noiselessly, I was in the wheelchair, started pushing me, we were leaving, fluorescents swayed back and forth, flickered, dancing shadows, muted hospital drama played out, nurses passed me, doctors, and a man pushing something, a short man (C▮▮▮▮l logo on the back of his shirt), he almost turned, and then noise came back in a flurry. I almost passed out in the dream; and I remember wondering, only vaguely aware it *was* a dream, what would happen if I passed out *in* a dream. Would I go somewhere else? But merely probing at this subreality caused a shift in the air—the atmosphere—followed by a static, a low wind

(*conchlike*)

---

[22] By then this "black substance" was growing under seven of my ten fingernails and it dribbled from my nose at least once a day (thus my checking the bathroom wastebasket—to see if it spread: it did); had it not been for this reporter's question, I would've kept making rationalizations, i.e., that I'd somehow smashed my hand, causing my fingertips to bruise; that my blood was just . . . unusually dark (actually just straight-up fucking black).

—and as the black man pushed me (was he supposed to be my father, whom I never met?) I grabbed the sleeve of a passing nurse, asked her, "Who is that man" (referring to the short guy walking away pushing something)?

She said, "███████████████████"

WHAT? Her words were blotted by black rot, and the conch was roaring a discordant melody of crab-clatter and waves and wind.

"He's a vendor for C██████l."

A VENDOR FOR WHAT? Trying to listen *through* the blackened rot of her words.

"*Cr███ell.*"

WHEN I WOKE UP I couldn't remember for what company the man was a vendor, nor why my subconscious mind thought it was important, nor what triggered it in the first place. I decided to abandon that thread of mystery altogether and instead to surf the web for the professorial-looking fella; I Googled the ████████ State Police personnel but got no bites. "Black lawyers" got significant search results, likely due to post–George Floyd algorithms that made lists like "the best Black lawyers in ████████" more visible: still nothing. I eventually gave up on finding this man, too, and called the only person I knew from ████████.

Unfortunately, I didn't have Detective Washington's personal cell—we weren't on *that* level—so I called the police department instead. A woman answered.

"Hi, there. I'm hoping to speak to Detective Washington."

"*Who?*"

"Washington. I never got his first name, sorry, but it's important" (at least for my own sensibilities—my own sanity—it was).

Papers ruffled. Muffled voices. Static. A low wi—

"*May I ask who's speaking.*"

"Trellis. Felix Trellis."

"*If this is a prank—*"

"—ma'am, this *is* Felix Trellis. And I'm not trying to be annoying or invasive, and I apologize if you're busy, but I would appreciate—really, *really* appreciate—if you were to transfer me to Detective Washington. He helped me out last year investigating the Lighthouse Killings. And if this is somehow an improper method for reaching him, could you please instruct me on the proper way? I really don't want to put you in a jam."

Silence.

I checked to see if she'd hung up. She hadn't. I was apparently just on mute. Then noise filtered back in and she said, "*Detective Washington is no longer with us.*"

"He quit?"

"*No.*" A beat. "*He passed away.*"

The floor fell from under me. My tingling lips moved and I heard myself say, "How did he pass?"

"*Are you* sure *you remember speaking to Detective Washington—and not Worchester or Williamston?*"

I paused, if only to make her think I was giving her question some thought, then I said, "No. It was definitely Washington. Why?"

"*It seems unlikely.*"

"Why?"

"*For the same reason he passed. Cancer. Of the lung. He was very sick, for like . . . half a year, I think . . . before he died—I mean, passed. Also . . . he was the responding officer on the night of . . . you know . . . the Lighthouse Killings—which is why I said 'it seems unlikely,' Mr. Trellis.*"

"How do you mean?"

She sighed. "*Another officer had to drag him off Rowling. Would have killed him if there hadn't been intervention. What I'm saying is, I doubt he'd have helped you prove Rowling's innocence.*"

"He was sick?"

"*Very.*"

"Are we sure we're talking about the *same* Detective Washington? Tall, beefy, mustache, a propensity for Hawaiian shirts, personality larger than life"—and I probably wouldn't have said what I said next if not for the contrast against my own ethnicity—"white."

"*Detective Washington was tall. But you're describing someone else. Washington was black*"—I almost blurted out "I KNEW IT," but held my tongue—"*not white. Sounds like you're talking about*"—did she stifle a laugh?—"*Ronald O'Connor Jr., though I don't see* why. *Well, I guess I do, but—no, I can't. Listen. I'm just a twenty-two-year-old desk officer. I'm trying to work my way up to detective before I'm thirty, and I don't want you to get me into—as you put it—some kind of jam. I can't say for a fact that the man you spoke to was Mr. O'Connor . . . but it sure does sound like him. If you told me he had a toothpick in his mouth, I'd pretty much confirm it.*"

I felt cold. The floor under my feet was swaying waterlike, teeming with

(*night*)

fish.

"Maybe I misremembered his name," I lied. "And maybe I only *thought* he was a cop. Could you at least tell me where I could find this Ronald guy?"

"*He's part of the school.*"

"Teacher? Janitor? Councilor?"

"*Not the* public *school. I'm talking about the School of Yahweh—in other words, he's a staff member at the*

Church of the Fish. That's really all I can say."
And that's all she *did* say; she hung up.

I SPENT NEARLY A WEEK collecting everything I could on ████████'s origins.

This entailed deep dives into:

(1) All public info on the Church of the Fish, including the staff—aka School—and, lo and behold, there was an article from *The Dagwood Journal* about a fundraiser "to end illiteracy." Kneeling between three grungy-looking kids was a mustachioed man sporting a button-up short-sleeve shirt depicting an apocalyptically tumultuous war between flamingos, palm trees, and coconuts. The caption read CHURCH VOLUNTEER RONALD O'CONNOR BRINGS LITERACY TO DISENFRANCHISED YOUTH).

(2) Charlie Blackwood and his wife Alma.

(3) Scientific research journals on organisms "similar," at least in appearance, to the *Sea Manna*, since none had published anything on the *Sea Manna* themselves[23]).

(4) Ron Ullman [Senior]'s *A Dark History of the Families of the Fish.* I also listened to most of his grandson's ("Wayward" Ron Ullman Jr.) podcasts (was unnerved to find that, as a child, he had described a big black shark in his grandparents' driveway, not dissimilar to my own psychedelic experience, on the night of his grandpar-

---

[23] Which gives me the feeling that the locals protect them, keep them, *possess* them, put them up on a divine pedestal.

ents' being murdered), researched articles on "The Charlotte Farmhouse Massacre," and read two of Wayward Ron's Axiom-published books—which built upon his grandfather's legacy by circuitously adding to ████████'s settlers' relation with the "peculiar" Native Americans whose tribe's name has been lost by the ceaseless grind of centuries (or by design).

(5) Obscure forums and other fringy website rabbit holes—such as the pseudonymous Gretchen Whitmer Is A Lizard Person's blog *Dark Alcoves of the Biosphere*, the most recent conspiratorial entry called "The Conspiracy of the Fish" . . .

. . . but all of this seemed only to show me the dark sheet of sea, and my research never armed me with the tools to discover what lay underneath its surface . . .

. . . and then I dreamt of the chasm again and the manuscript at its throat. For the first time I went even *deeper* into the dream. I hadn't just passively read from it—I'd actually gone *into* it; swallowed wholly. The infinite darkhouse stood tranquilly before a finite manikin called Felix Trellis; and then, after enduring my manikin's trek into the mouth of that stony creature (wanting to turn back but unable to deter my dream vessel's trajectory), I discovered, after the desk spat me out, I had written the whole account somnambulantly.

I immediately went out onto my balcony and burnt the pages with my Zippo. I watched the flapping, flaming flecks swim into the cool, pre-sunrise dark. As I relay this to you now, you must understand that the descriptions in those pages are too despairing—unholy, even—to attempt replicating from memory. But even if I could, my decision not to is my way of sparing you from such miseries.

———

LATER THAT DAY I EMAILED GWIALP via his contact information on the *Dark Alcoves* weblog, hoping it was up to date. I knew that a "real" journalist wouldn't touch this story—primarily because it didn't have an ending yet, but also because it was either too fantastic, too dangerous, too politically divisive, or too enticing. If the latter, he might want to come to ██████████—but I couldn't allow anyone else getting hurt or getting dead, not after what happened to John R. Francis.

Or me.

What festered inside my bathroom wastebasket—born from toilet paper drenched in my black-blood snot—was evidence enough to prove some askew nefariousness pertaining to ████████, the Church of the Fish, or some oblique entity just barely outside my psychic periphery. Based on GWIALP's blog, I knew he would take the necessary precautions. Plus, someone had already targeted him—likely for the same reasons *they* went after Ron Ullman Sr., Rowan Esko, and (the real) Brian Maxwell, and then John R. Francis, me, and Hector Rowling. All that being said, I think they—whoever *they* might be—merely warned GWIALP and his followers, passive-aggressively threatening them to stay away from ████████. Whether via protectiveness or sacredness or public safety[24], I know not.

EVERYTHING YOU'VE READ SO FAR, including this part, I've put on a flash drive. In case GWIALP doesn't follow through—or gets *got* by whoever these persons (or *non-*

———

[24] You'll understand this latter "working hypothesis" via various attached documents.

persons) are—I'll give it to the only trustworthy person I know (who won't try to stop me): the janitor of my apartment complex, a man in his mid-thirties named Sam Kunkel, a self-described "enthusiastic antitheist." I'll tell him, "If I don't come back in two weeks, by November 15th, then send this out to anyone and everyone—websites, news, magazines, YouTubers." I imagine he'll agree on the basis of "giving those cult nuts what they deserve."

I fear if I told both Sam and GWIAP I wouldn't be back for an absolute fact (which I believe is an absolute fact), or at least not "back" with a heartbeat, they might misinterpret my declaration as suicidal ideation and call the police—as my therapist had.

Anyway, this is my last entry.

I want to be in ██████████ when the *Sea Manna* washes ashore; be there for the festival; and use 324 to open the safe—lest I'm consumed by that which dwells in or beneath the town. Or by the town itself.

"Oh. And Sam?" I'll say after handing him the flash drive.

"Yes, boss?" he might say back.

"Just in case you or a neighbor *smell* something— or have some kind of instinct even if you don't smell anything—don't go into my apartment; and if you do go inside, don't go into my bathroom; and if you *do* go into my bathroom, wear a hazmat suit."

Maybe a crucifix, too.

I'LL ALSO GIVE SAM KUNKEL a letter I wrote to my therapist, Dr. Thawlen—with strict instructions not to deliver it to her until after two weeks.

———

DEAR READER, I'll tell you the curtailed version of what I wrote to my therapist: If you're reading this, I'm probably dead.

SOURCE OF MYSTERIOUS ODOR REVEALED

By **Skip M. E. Ozark**
10/28/22

In a gripping turn of events, renowned journalist Jonathon Reilly Francis, presumed to have met an untimely demise last year, was discovered "newly deceased" on his patio on October 20th, 2022. The discovery came about when concerned neighbors, drawn by "strange chanting" and "a putrid odor," ventured to investigate the origin of the sound and smell.

Elliot Maverick—a lifelong friend as well as the esteemed lawyer of the late Francis—is poised to deliver a more detailed statement to shed some light on this revelation.

It has come to our attention, however, leaked by a reliable source, that John R. Francis has been under protective services since his initial involvement in reexamining the Lighthouse Killings (predating Felix Trellis's involvement by a month). It's unknown at this point in time if Mr. Francis was involved in the Rowling retrial.

On Twitter, October 26, Elliot Maverick let slip in a

response to alt-right incel conspiracist GWIALP (standing for: Gretchen Whitmer [Michigan governor] is a Lizard Person) that his client and friend, John R. Francis, had been consistently harassed for leaving the town of ▮▮▮▮ ▮▮▮▮ by the man (Brian Maxwell) who had contracted him—then later contracted Felix Trellis, of now considerable fame after winning a Pulitzer Prize for Investigative Journalism—to write an article "to prove Hector Rowling's innocence."

GWIALP immediately instigated by claiming that someone had already murdered Brian Maxwell and staged it as a shark attack, that the person who hired Francis was "merely impersonating Maxwell," and that Maverick needed to get his facts straight before "tarnishing the character of a man who can't defend himself."

Maverick responded back: ". . . evidence suggests no foul play regarding Maxwell. He got drunk, swam in the ocean, passed out, was shark food—end of discussion."

GWIALP does mention in this heated, controversial Twitter feud the discovery of another body in a similar "condition"—referring to a Native man, his head and legs eaten (presumably by a shark), found washed ashore ten miles upcoast. However, there are only a few anecdotal bits of validation via eyewitnesses and testimony—id est, no photographs, no police report, nothing whatsoever.

To find the entire thread, click <u>here.</u>

What do you guys think? Is this just a social contagion of mass hysteria? Are these things connected? How was Francis being harassed? And why did he commit suicide? Or (GWIALP must be rubbing off on me) was it not suicide?

Please stay tuned.

[Photo depicts blue-haired thirty-year-old male posing in front of bookshelf]

Caption: **Jonathon Reilly Francis, columnist for *GQ, Time,* and *Entertainment Weekly***

PHARMA GIANT CR█████ELL AIDS IN █████████ STATE PRISON QUARANTINE

By **Asha Reese**
10/30/22

As of Saturday, October 27th, officials confirmed only two casualties, inmate Yuri Reed and prison guard Trey Gomez, after the ███████ State Prison personnel find in its facility a rare and aggressive variant of Leptospirosis. In a press release Warden William Quin expressed deep gratitude toward pharmaceutical conglomerate Cr████ell for "their swift support."

[Photo depicts a middle-aged, balding white man, wearing a burgundy sports jacket, shaking hands with a black man in a black business suit]

Caption: **Warden William Quin and Cr███ell response team supervisor**

A BEARDED BLACK MAN SITS on an office chair, wearing a loose, stonewashed *Dragon Ball Z* shirt. Around his neck a crucifix necklace glistens dully in the ugly fluorescence of the room. Eyes bloodshot; dark, sleepless circles sit beneath. For one second he just sits there, then two, three, four and five. Six seconds. Can we hear something in the background? The sound of wind or waves or something else—something nefariously *conch-like*?

Splashed against his back, upon the wall, is an array of newspaper cutouts, printed articles, photographs (a lighthouse; a statue of two men and a woman; a coastal town; a coast; a black-and-white portrait of men and women, all wearing fish masks, standing in front of a building; a blue-haired man), sticky notes, notebook pages with scrawls (we can barely make out the emboldened words sloppily spread across three sheets:

> the inviolate structure: cyclopean, darkly
> sleeping, and always but never or sometimes
> encroaching like an enigmatic organism made of
> stone and clay or bone and blood or the residue
> of a god's ghost. Or an amalgamation—a

<u>convergence</u>—of everythingness. Of nothing. Just a void. An oblivion. Or a beacon—a reliquary—<u>for</u> not only the things—vacuous emissaries—or *thing*—the GREAT DOVE/GOD'S HAND—in the void but the essence of VACUITY itself, the soul of black itself, DAG ELOHIM: the calling not *from* the void but *of the void*),

magnified passages (of a philosophical nature), and a crucifix with a fish pinned to it instead of Jesus of Nazareth.

Fifteen seconds drift by.

The man inhales deeply. When he exhales, it sounds like an overheated teapot. He opens his mouth, hesitates, licks his lips, opens his mouth again, then snaps his head back. A dark-colored rash is observable at the bottom of his throat. Rigidly he cranes his neck, tilts up his head, listens.

"I was wrong about Francis's media."

Contorting his body, he reaches into his sweatpants' pocket and pulls out a phone.

"I should have paid more attention to the time-codes."

He taps the phone and a voice begins: "*. . . my client, and friend, was merely waiting for the storm to settle, for the harassment to stop—no, a better way of describing it is something like this: the* ▆▆▆▆▆▆▆ *locals relentlessly terrorized my client like a gaggle of bigoted thugs. They were trying to silence him. To make sure his story wouldn't get out. In fact, on his first day there, a group of people had followed him during his investigation, gone so far as to knock him to the ground and cut open his arm with a machete. So he left town, then Mr. Maxwell kept harassing him, threatening him. So my client went*

*so far as to stage his own death. Then went into protec-
tive—"*

Audio pauses.

"Which means . . . which means that the scream—
Francis's scream—during the interview with Esko—and
I double-checked the timecode on the audio file and the
video, just to be certain beyond a reasonable doubt—
well, his scream happened *after* the lighthouse. Obviously they were trying to just scare him away by cutting
his arm. Or maybe not—I've got my working hypothesis
regarding their true motivations. Anyway. Regardless of
their motivations, Francis didn't leave—he went to
Rowan Esko's sometime later.

"So I'm going to break into Esko's house to figure
out what caused Francis to scream, what made Esko—
a man who'd been physically handicapped—to go
through the trouble of wheeling himself over to wherever
Francis had put his recorder and press the stop button.

"The only thing I know for certain is that Esko may
have had some . . . well, maybe not *reprehensible* motives, but at least 'ulterior' ones.

"He certainly wasn't in cahoots with the black-van
people. He knew about them, seemed nervous about
them, but maybe it was because Francis was there. Obviously Esko wasn't aware of Francis's previous encounter with the black-van people, and Francis probably
didn't know the people who attacked him even *had* a
black van. Or maybe—concerning my hypothesis—maybe the black-van people were already keeping an eye on
Esko for an . . . *adjacently related reason.*

"But then it begs the question of how faux-Maxwell
and -Washington—aka Ronald O'Connor Jr.—add into
the mix . . . I need some fresh air."

He disappears from the frame.

Muffled footfalls.

A transference of light and shadow.
The many pinned-up sheets flutter about to the wall.
Coughing.
Off-camera: "*. . . and the* Sea Manna *have yet to arrive. I would very much like to see them, before . . .*"
Indecipherable mutter.
Webcam jiggles.
End of file.

NOW THE MAN IS CLEAN-shaven. Wearing a light blue button-up. With labored breathing he says, "Last night the first *Sea Manna* were reported to have washed ashore. I'd like to take a look at one before going to Esko's. Then the lighthouse."

He holds up his hands; they're shaking uncontrollably. "I don't think I'll be writing anything else—" He coughs. "My hands are shot . . . my fingers are there, I see them, I do, but they're . . . *gone*. Everything's swimming around. So from this point on I'll be using this camera"—he unsteadily points to a button on his shirt—"and"—with great difficulty, he manages to pull out and lift his phone—"this for recording audio. Every ten minutes, both the footage and audio files will automatically go to the cloud."

A beat.

A sound permeates the motel room, something not unlike a—

THE SWALLOWED TOWN (II)

—A

(*crab-*)

clatter; a conch shell pressed against your ear—whistling, humming; and a scream—your scream—and the waves crashing against the rocks farther up the beach; and a pyre, great and fiery red and orange and yellow and blue, and hot hot hot, casting shadows of dark gods and gods even older than the dark—*anteabyssum*, as it were—and darker than it, too; and their demonstrative shades—or *Their* shades—mayhap T HEIR shades—made of black and dull orange and yellow—flicker across the sand, reach into the sea, and press their/Their/T HEIR shadowy incarnations into the undulating waters, stirring it, teasing it.

It's frothing, the sea is.

Alive.

And the fire: your eyes go back to it, and the dark effigies separate themselves from the rumbling inferno. There, Margaret Radon's niece Sarah is cradling her famine-dead babe in a wool blanket. There, three skeletal kids are sitting on a fallen tree, eyes hungry. There, a consortium of crabs dances in the twilight. There, your husband—short in stature, tall of forehead, pale of skin, large of eyes—stands at the mouth of the blaze, and when someone calls out *"Malefica!"* as you're dragged across the freezing wet sand and the cutting sea-chewed stones, his eyes dart to the insulter—

Resulting in abrupt and stark silence.

"I'm sorry, my Alma," he tells you as you're placed before him. "But nothing *wrong* is going to happen."

Then why all this?

"It's less than what is truly called for, I believe," he says elusively, enigmatically. And after a spell of silence, save for the wind and the waves and the wood-licking flames and the clattering of the crabs, he adds, "But I must have hope that *this* will suffice, that the Fish—"

"Dag Elohim," says one of the shadows—you think it's Fredrick Grayson's father, a former rabbi-turned-priest.

"Dag Elohim," repeat several others.

"—yes," says your sweet Charlie, *"Dag Elohim.* We must believe that IT is, um, *just.* Yeah, and *understanding."*

What is wrong with you? Your eyes. Your skin. Your stench. Your words.

"I'm enlightened. The *Manna* have shown me a great many things."

I'm your wife, Charles Blackwood!

"No, I was merely a placeholder for SOMETHING GREATER. You never took my name. You've never even bedded me, but I—um, yes—I never pried, and I don't blame you. We both know the reasons why. And I was proud to be called yours through ritual, though not by name. But all is forgiven now. All of it is for a, um, yeah, a reason *beyond* our understanding—

"Behold!"

You beheld.

From where a water- and fire-reflecting rockface drank from a mouth of jagged teeth a torrent of high tide, there comes a sound of low wind like a conch shell pressed against your ear—and something disturbs the darkness of the cave. It's so black the night is blinding in comparison, and its movement so smooth that as it hovers across the wet sand, the driftwood, and the dancing, clattering, worshiping crabs, you hope against all hope that it's a shadow spilled from a passing-over cloud.

But you know it isn't, so you turn away.

"I give her—whom I've set aside and prepared for THY consummation, oh GREAT ONE—to THEE. And I denounce my name—Charles Blackwood. I was with the land, of the wood, but now of the sea. I have thus have cast an anchor, have moored myself; I *was* Charles Blackwood, but *now* have become Charles Blackmoor: an apostle of the GREAT ONE whose stripped-away flesh you have offered to me to satiate my soul, to cleanse it; apostate of the OLD WAYS, I offer a *pure* companion."

You look skyward as the superblack is almost upon you.

But something pulls away your gaze.

At the top of the sea-facing rockface, where the tall grass and the wildflowers sway back and forth in the wind, a

tether

spire

umbilical cord

thing you can't understand stretches itself to the moon. A string of blood, a song of songs, and a deeper kind of

 is he awake

 he's been in and out wait usually
 Richard is our C█████l vendor are you
 filling in for him I don't think I've seen

*you around   but I don't think I've ever
seen Richard take a day off*

yes he's um fallen ill I'm afraid

do you know him

Richard

No   him   in room ▮

(*lust*)
love. You weep at the inviolate structure—at the **darkhouse**—where your broods will flourish and for a-
many generations walk its halls.
"Do you take Dag Elohim" *to be your husband.*
"I" *do not, oh* ▮, *I'm sorry I'm sorry I'm sorry, I see
reflected off the face of the waters the very Devil, the face
of my Charles, oh* ▮ *forgive me.*
"It's too late to repent" *you've been selected.*
"Oh ▮! Oh ▮! Charles, why" *are you
doing this?*
"To transcend from a finite note in a, um—a ballad
of meat and flesh. To instead become quasi-infinite like
the ORPHANS OF THE ATERCOSM. To see ANTERIOR
SKIES and listen to" *THEIR SONG. Shhhh. IT's here. You
may kiss the bride.*

Thou becomest words in *The Second Book of Jonah;*
thou becomest its bedrock; thou becomest its mo▮;
thou becomest like a sound of wind, like the low
rumble—mayhap a *whisper*—of a conch shell pressed
against an ears. Mayhap that ear belongs to a man.

Mayhap one day that man—that traveler who unknowingly slinks across the residual memory of some
LONESOME GREAT DREAMER—who hears your song—
finds himself at one of the very few extraholy *compitum*

on *terra*, the LUNARIS DEVERSORIUM; and mayhap that

> *lonesome hotel; vacant land of solid,*
> *rough, hot, black stone enclosing it, where*
> *metal carriages come to sleep; baked by a*
> *red sun or moon or eye*

(*oh open up now Alma it burns but for a moment*)
man watches you now through a window in a room. And there, on his chair, unable to move, mayhap he sees Fredrick Grayson and Margaret Radon's husband, Ethan, grab each of your wrists and stretch you out; and mayhap watches also as your husband approaches you with a blade made of driftwood and conch shell, mumbling unconscious "ums" and "yeses." He presses into your breast the blade and says also "May she be the MOTHER OF MATANAH NE'EVAH and bring forth the SOLEMNITY OF DAG ELOHIM, amen." And then the man, whose skin is like the night invading the dancing flames, sheds a tear into the foaming sea by your feet.

Then the shadow bears upon you.

Fredrick and Ethan pull harder.

Your husband digs in and presses down down down the shell, ripping ripping ripping—

"Witch," yells a boy. "Witch," yells a girl. "Bitch," yells Margaret Radon.

You gasp. The conch-blade breaks into your lungs and is reborn; jagged and sharp, and down and down and down and through and through and "OH ██████!" you yell, and the dark man watching you—transfixed upon you—can't turn away as your screams become raspy and soft, almost like a low wind, like pressing one's ear up to a—

You see him.

Your prophet.

You look right into the shadow that swallows you—

you look *through* it—at he who blends into the night, his beautiful exotic skin—glistening with sweat and seawater—such as it is. And there you are.

Some place.

Some time.

A strange dress flowing halfway down your thigh, and around you are people dressed just as strangely, as *scantily.*

Disembodied, twangy music overhead: you wonder where it comes from. It will haunt you until your dying breath, those magic hymns with no mouths singing and no hands playing instruments.

Unearned knowledge flows through you, and you look up and see the exotic man who'd been watching you and your mania-festering family and friends prepare to sacrificially terminate you. He's dressed differently now, clean-shaven. Your mouth finds words to say, but someone else makes you say them. *Was I wrong?* you think. *Is* ██ *using me despite my rebellion?* But you can't feel ██, if there ever had been one —black blots out the name. You can only feel the presence of the Devil.

"Do you know ██ has plans for you?" you say to the man who'd been watching you from a dream. Then you taste the sea and the dream finds its home. Then someone—*something*—slips inside your spirit, causing everything—time and space, reality and illusion—to unravel, to shuffle, to slip backward and forward and side to side, filling you up with a sulphuric rottenness, a salty bloatedness, and a

(*different kind of*)

blackness; and now you stand in the shade of a tree in a wood of a strange eon. Your naked, swollen foot presses on a fallen branch you hadn't known you were stepping on until it snaps. A movement draws your attention toward a man—your prophet—at the entrance of a peculiar house across a patch of land where inexplicable iron machines lie strewn about. He'd heard you so turns and glances at where you're trapped in the dark, in the tides of time. He squints at you—*through* you—and turns as the door before him opens, revealing to you, beyond your prophet, a small man who steps into a sliver of light, which discards his cruel silhouette like a snakeskin: it is he who has swum through the sea of time whose surface reflected his very own face—

"Charles?"

FOUND FOOTAGE IS CONFIRMED A HOAX!
BasedNews

"Fish Files" released by QAnon-friendly internet conspiracist Gretchen Whitmer is a Lizard Person is "unreadable fantasy," says CNN contributor.
TRU GateMedia

Famous Journalist Felix Trellis still missing; FBI-sequestered laptop files being processed.
Fox News

Alex Jones and Wayward Ron talk about his family growing up in ██████████, GWIALP's "Fish Files," Hector Rowling's relatedness to Ron, and the possible extraterrestrial origins of the SEA MANNA.
Globber Buy is Dyslexic

On Gorgon Podcast, Tyler Rosenboom—aka GWIALP—claims his name came about as sarcastic-tinged hyperbole and has no association with QAnon despite some coincidental overlap.
Conservative Daily

Hollywood SFX professional says "creature" in the Felix Trellis found footage is the best "deepfake" out there.
Lib Cake Media

Felix Trellis' residence—a Sharp Point, Illinois, apartment complex—is quarantined. Cr███ell hazmat crew seen with body bags. Mainstream media calling people who connect this with ███████ State Prison quarantine, where Hector Rowling was incarcerated, as "tinfoil-hatters."
FerretSlippers.Net

Cr███ell CEO, Dr. Yukon Seagrave Jr., and infectious disease expert, Dr. Kenji Yamamoto, discuss strange variant of Leptospirosis. They conclude: "Deadly <u>but</u> with a very low infection rate."
Bio World

Wayward Ron received raw "Fish Files" documents, reportedly writing new novel called "The Swallowed Town and Other Rabbit Holes You Should Avoid."
FerretSlippers.Net

John R. Francis's boyfriend being rushed to hospital spawns even more whacky "far-right" conspiracies.
TRU GateMedia

Twitter, Instagram, Facebook, and Reddit unite in censoring "Fish Files"-related material pertaining to specific locations. One inside source claims it's a public safety concern, another source suggests

it's to prevent "religious maltreatment" of the Children of the Fish."
Fox News

TIME set to publish a reportedly "thought-provoking, edgy" Ron Ullman Jr.-penned article carefully analyzing the found footage. Ullman says it "might be a chapter in his upcoming novel 'The Swallowed Town.'" *TIME* Senior Editor deflects controversy, saying "QAnon connection is unconvincing; [the story] should be culturally neutral, politically bilateral, and its investigation is communally beneficial."
CNN

Ron Ullman Jr. set to release what *Rolling Stone* calls his "magnum opus . . . a triumphant, unnerving investigation into what may be the most polarizing, mystifying, and creepiest work of nonfiction . . . his personal connection to this story elevates *The Swallowed Town* to a transcendent, plateau-shattering level in the true crime genre (if you could call it that)."
Book Royale

In an exclusive interview, Ron Ullman Jr. says he refused to step foot into his father's hometown, ██████████, when researching his upcoming release called *The Swallowed Town and Other Rabbit Holes You Should Avoid* (based on the controversial "Fish Files").
Fox News

Richard Spangley (C██████ l vendor and ████ ████ local) found dead in maintenance closet at ████████ Hospital "in a state of undress." Nurse spoke to a man claiming to be Mr. Spangley's fill-in, "But the Crim-Cell outfit he wore looked way too big."

Police say hospital surveillance footage appears to be "tampered with"—they have no leads.

Please call (███) ███-███ if you have any information.
████████████ **Local News**

"Ron Ullman Jr.'s sixth novel transcends anything he's done previously. From a gut-wrenching examination—no, *dissection*—of Felix Trellis's early life (his
mother's admission to a psychiatric ward when he was
only six and his father's working three jobs to provide
for the family; his younger sister's suicide; his own
struggles with alcohol and cocaine in his early twenties)
to the harrowing and terrifying final moments prior to
his disappearance, *The Swallowed Town & Other Rabbit
Holes You Should Avoid* is a character study as much as
it is a true crime as much as it is a deep-dive into some
strange, unanswerable mystery."   5/5

—Big Red Reviews

"Ron Ullman Jr.'s most personal novel yet. A *tour de
force*."   4/5

—TIME

"One of the most pretentious novels my eyes have ever
had the torturous task of attempting to read. I think
maybe the Lighthouse Killings (Hector Rowling's mother
being a blood-relative to Ron), not to mention The Charlotte Farmhouse Massacre, has made this story *too*

personal for conspiracist Wayward Ron. Also, he tried way too hard to emulate Capote's *In Cold Blood* by spending copious amounts of time getting to know Felix Trellis's and John R. Francis's early life.

"Cosmic horror—which is, ladies and gentlemen, what this novel is—works best with a 'cold' narrative. Otherwise it teeters into gothic literature. And *yeah yeah yeah*, 'But this is a true story!' some of you might be saying, to which I respond, with an eyeroll, 'Yeah, "sure" it is.'

"What's frustrating is that stories 'Based on True Events' actually *do* have plenty of freedom to be creative, but by the time Ullman does anything innovative—his last few chapters, which (especially the interview with Massie and Yvonne) *are* genuinely creepy—I'd already clocked out.

"For this to be a five-star for me, he should have cut out all the melodramatic fat of superfluous family life and focused exclusively on the Festival of the Fish, The Church of the Fish, the black van, the men in black, and the Hector Rowling case.

"As a True Crime with a cosmic horror/occult tilt, *The Swallowed Town* excels. But it's bogged down with too much fluff.   2/5."

—Grumpy Review Dude

"One of the most bigoted, anti-Native propaganda books I've ever read. Completely misrepresents Natives to even *suggest* a 'fringe tribe' worships or protects or whatever-it-is-he-is-or-isn't-implying a fictional Fish Monster. That's absolutely insane (yeah, we are talking about Wayward Ron, who's friends with Alex Jones, so I shouldn't be *that* surprised) and there's no evidence that this tribe even existed, and if you say that that is by design, you are part of the tinfoil-hat-wearing problem.

If the extraordinary claim is that it's 'based on a true story,' there needs to be extraordinary evidence—ESPE-CIALLY if it is of a borderline-racist, even if only *obliquely* or *accidentally*, proclivity. You should not read this racist book. Do not give Wayward Ron a plat-form."   1/5

—Malarey Q

"Wait so who wuz fake maxwell whwat wuz the point of the cop dude w/ the toothpick am i missing something otherwise i liked the footnotes n how we got alot of diff angels of the lagoon monstrosity from the news."
     3/5

—Amazon Reviewer

"I bought this book for my husband, and he loved it."
     5/5

—Amazon Reviewer

"Racist book. Do not read."   1/5

—Amazon Reviewer

"Wayward Ron is spreading hate. I don't recommend."
     1/5

—Amazon Reviewer

"Listen. I'm a Native American, and I can assure you that there is nothing racist about Ullman's *The Swallowed Town*. I remember Dan Simmons getting similar pushback for his book *The Terror* because it just so happened that his main antagonist had participated in homosexual sex—therefore that meant that Simmons was saying that only terrible people are gay or that gay people are terrible. I don't subscribe to that. Or in *Resident Evil 5*, that CAPCOM was racist for having an African village of infected black people (nobody batted an eye in *Resident Evil 6* when the Chinese city had exclusively Asian zombies—but I digress).

"My point being: just because Ullman theorizes that a Native American tribe has possibly been 'worshiping' or 'defending' a fish deity and may have committed some murders—such as his grandparents'—does NOT mean he's saying that ALL NATIVE AMERICANS ARE MURDERERS.

"There's a lot of nuance, and I think most of you people who are review-bombing this book have not actually read it. If you had, you'd have noticed the second theory:

"That the Native American tribe has been containing and preventing an outbreak from spreading. That's why they were waiting for Hector when he was released from prison; they knew he was infected.

"That's why they didn't kill John R. Francis. They cut his arm, did a blood test, saw that he wasn't infected, let him go—but he didn't leave town, interviewed Esko, got infected, and then ran away, elaborately staged his own death, infected his boyfriend, and burnt himself alive via disease-riddled brain.

"I also believe that's why they chased down Felix Trellis: they wanted to make sure he wasn't infected. It must be there are certain places in town that are 'hot spots' for infection—the lighthouse, some of the old houses, and probably the 'Sea Manna' themselves (nobody is allowed to capture any—dead or alive—probably because they're infectious).

"That being said, while it wasn't 'racist' like the bombers are saying, it also wasn't as good as the critics are saying. Lots of loose ends, including Faux-Maxwell (who was he? What was his motive?), Ronald O'Connor Jr. (why did he pretend to be a cop?), and what role does The Keeper have in The Church of the Fish?"   3/5

—Amazon Reviewer

"Reading this is like being assaulted by a posse of people all wearing cheap Alex Jones Halloween masks and wielding hard rubber swords shaped liked monstrous phalluses in a Louisiana bayou as they ride orcas having somehow adapted to freshwater—yet, despite the weirdness and discomfort (or maybe *because* of the weirdness and the discomfort), you kind of enjoy it. But you can't tell anyone about the experience, or the enjoyment of the experience, because they'll think you're weird and disown you."   4/5

—Amazon Reviewer

"To many big words I had to look up. To many big cententses I couldnt understand. To many big paraglyphs I felt I felt a stroke going to happen. Go see a head doctor if you liked this book. So boring end confusing." 1/5

—Amazon Reviewer

"Opened package this morning, one day after it was supposed to arrive. Front upper-left corner of the cover was bent. NOT HAPPY!"   1/5

—Amazon Reviewer

"Ron Ullman's writing style is so pompous. The opening paragraph in Chapter 1 specifically comes to mind—it's too long, weird, antiquated, and narcissistic (this book isn't even about him, but he somehow managed to simultaneously throw a pity party and show off his 'writing abilities'), with too many big or flat-out made-up words. It was exhausting to read. It felt like reading Lovecraft on LSD—like, he was on LSD when he wrote it and I was on LSD when I read it; it's a full-on double whammy of psychedelic, highbrow, (very) old-fashioned, literary-prose nonsense. Like, we're talking 3 or 4 pages long—the paragraph is that long. Yeah. The editor should be fired from Axiom. Also, the cherry on top—and further evidence the editor was sleeping on the job and didn't look at this convoluted megaparagraph more carefully—there are two periods at the end. If this typo were ANYWHERE else, it wouldn't have bothered me as much. But c'mon, Ullman, just write like a normal human being."   2/5

—Amazon Reviewer

"You will all be swallowed by Dag Elohim."   5/5

—Amazon Reviewer

. . . DREAMT LAST NIGHT THAT I was ten years old. My parents—whom I'm ashamed to say in my middle age have lost their definitions in my memory, but the spirit of my dream had resurrected them in a near-perfect recreation—had taken me to ███████ for the Festival of the Fish (which I've never actually attended because my grandparents and father had moved away before I was even an inkling of a possibility—and after this dream, I think I never will). I quickly realized upon arriving at the nautical town—where the buildings, touched with notes of medievalness, had about them a festering uncanniness; where, beyond the trees to the west of town, I could see the arch of a rudimentary Ferris wheel (the wind made it *groan*) and glimpses of some anemic roller-coaster snaking through the trees (the wind made it *hiss*); where the streets were lined with vacant vendor tents and foodless food trucks—that something was off. That an off-putting aura permeated from unseen chasms just outside my periphery. That my dream-insight allowed me to see a lingering deposit about the town—where, through the fabric of all the atoms of all there was to see and hear and smell and touch and taste, danced hazy ontological patterns of chaos and order, Night and Day, and death, and a juncture of death: a liminal metamorphosis not quite its final form, wholly imperceptible and cerebrally impenetrable. Overpowered and in awe, I quickly turned to find Mom's hand . . . but she was gone . . . so was Dad . . . and, too, were all the local Celebrants of the Fish. But I think they were *always* gone—husks of a memory of a town. I was, for all intents and purposes, alone in that Godless place. Except I didn't *feel* alone, at least not in the negative, and when I treaded farther through the deserted marine-decay-scented streets I found the shore to that seemingly never-ending gulf. My feet took me to its eerily still brine. I looked left and right and found a looming light-house breathing from its cyclopean eye inverted light—*black light*—whose ax-slain denizens nary flickered through my dreaming encephalon. Nor did I recall that both my parents, when I was ten, were sleeping in a state of deep decay beneath slabs of stone—and that my grandparents were either already similarly slain, as the Rowlings had been, or would be before my eleventh birthday; in fact, as I write this, tapping these melancholy-imbued letters on the keyboard of this MacBook cluttered with hundreds of digital dust-bunny-accumulating, time-moldering works of literature (both fiction and nonfiction; finished, mostly finished, and utterly abandoned), I think the dream, in a strange sort of darkened shell of an unborn eon—or dream-anchored alternative reality, not so different from Trellis's "Swallowed Town"—took place on the same exact day that my grandparents were killed. And then I looked out into that vacuous obsidian sea . . . out there, staring back at me, emanating an apotheosis of destitution and hyperdecay—perhaps antidecay—a Promethean feast of aborted, Godless monstrosities—*Leviathans*—whose veil between me (and *this* plane) and those forms of primordial chaos oozing from the fringes of our supposedly quantifiable world was but a Neoplatonic, rainbow-colored mist hovering above the waters like a contractually-agreed-upon axiomatic barrier. Looking away from that unromantic, ill-lit vista (I couldn't bear it any longer) and back toward the beach and the lighthouse, I found that my feet had drifted from the shore, the lighthouse now a white bottle and the rockface below it nothing but a dark, jagged stone in my grandparents' garden; and I found that the trees were like toothpicks with green parasites atop— moveless—and the town, separated from the hungry sea by the woods, appeared as if it were a long-neglected toy set belonging to some spoiled child. My little boy's feet began to tread through that ankle-deep, lukewarm water (which I now realize was saliva of some nearby creature, but the dream-child me wasn't aware of it . . . perhaps rationally so). A stench behind me. Something like meat moldering in a forgotten wet place for centuries. But I kept running running running. Water cascading in every direction. Sky darkening. The stars sighed across the heavens and then sizzled for a moment before winking out, leaving me in a strange *antilight*. I then realized without the articulated verbiage that I was not necessarily metaphorically, but perhaps metaliterally, in an ultranarcissistic god's "decaying fantasy," one which dwells in some outer darkness; or, feasibly, the quasi-immaterial combination—*code*, even—of antipersonality and antiego of the aforementioned's—i.e., the metaliteral, vacuous abyss's—*very deep and insanely deprived subconscious.* So much so, and so rottenly dark, so predatorial (perhaps *territorial,* if one were to ill-advisedly empathize with [and reduce] its nature), that it seeps—it *weeps!*—through reality, parasitically gnawing at its *genius loci,* its beacon of light, its *Ohr,* like bugs drawn to a lantern in darkness. And I knew—as I ran with a fervent, unsettling plerophory—that if I'd turned around and faced that presence whose slaver splattered about my tide-slicing feet, the ancient dark would have removed me from this world..

Then I woke up.

Here I am at my desk.

A cup of coffee by my side.

The jagged, enkindled eye of my cigar smoldering: a red-orange glow in the dark of my study.

A wind outside, low, ominous, and yes—*conchlike*: a whisper from the VOID . . .

I RETURN TO A PLACE to where I've never been, through the mind and memory of Felix Trellis, whose whereabouts are still unknown. We begin on November 7th, circa 2022, according to the timecode of the footage from the small camera—something you might imagine in a spy-thriller—inserted through the buttonhole of his button-up. It's important to note that when he walks up to his truck, the motion appropriately jittery but discernible, we see his reflection (that's not to say that someone hasn't swapped out or doctored the rest of the footage; yet I choose to believe in its authenticity). It's also important to point out that the camera doesn't record sound—for that, he's using a separate audio-capture app on his phone.

Ten minutes and thirty-five seconds later, he steps out of his truck and we see an intimidating brick house. The Esko estate, built in the late 1800s. Amos Esko (Rowan's uncle), Gabriel Rowling (Hector's great-grandfather), and my own grandfather had spent much of their youth there—specifically in a treehouse tucked within a great oak. They'd played an array of boyish games throughout the surrounding four and a half acres. I half see my grandfather's ghost darting around the corner of the brick quasi-mansion, two small shades fluttering after him, as Felix makes his way through the yard.

The windows are boarded. Yellow caution tape crisscrosses in an X about the front door, and even at this distance we're able to read a big white placard pasted at the caution tape's intersection—red-lettered, bold:

DO
NOT
ENTER

Though the footage is shaky, we're able to see the looming lighthouse in the background; and though the audio is assaulted by ruffling fabric and thrashing wind, we're are able to hear cawing seagulls and the crashing waves a mile away.

When Felix spins in a circle I can only imagine it's because he's looking for a black van. There is none (I've analyzed this portion of the footage to be comprehensively certain of this fact), so he continues his former trajectory. The front door is locked, but after five minutes of investigating the perimeter he's able to find an unlocked window and use, on the crisscrossing boards, a crowbar we don't even know he's holding until he brings it into frame.

"Why did Francis scream?" The question he asks

himself is a reference to Francis's own "found footage" (also in my possession). It seems as though he's asking *me*. And considering he'd instructed infamous conspiracist-blogger GWIALP to send the files to me, perhaps he was.

While our protagonist slides through the side-yard-facing window, I would like us to take a trip to Rosemont, California for a spell.

YOU WOULDN'T EXPECT, at least not upon the narrative of the mainstream media, that the lean and muscular twenty-six-year-old Massie Quinn (no surprise learning she's a CrossFit enthusiast) and her friend Yvonne Marilyn (neither would you be surprised to learn they'd met in CrossFit) had been so disturbed on the night of October 19th—the day *before* their agreed-upon investigation, only after dragging in Yvonne's boyfriend—that neither could sleep until exhaustion stole them around the Devil's hour.

I ask them: *why hadn't you thought to call the police?*

"I mean, we did," says Yvonne.

They exchange glances.

"I mean . . . *technically* I did," says Yvonne. "My boyfriend—Jamal—is a cop. I called him. Then, after we saw what we saw, he called his department and they sent other cops; and he's the one who mostly spoke to reporters and other people."

Other people? I press.

"Well," Yvonne continues, a finger combing her curly black hair, "just people." I can't help but notice her subsequent (though subtle) behavior: nervous fidgeting, strange facial expressions, wall-watching.

You haven't said much, Massie. What happened when Yvonne called her boyfriend? Why did it take till the next day for him to come?

Laughter—genuine, robust laughter from Massie. "This is *California*, man. We're not, you know, too far from that Bohemian Grove place—the one that that one tinfoil-hat-wearing nut snuck into—sorry, I didn't mean"—passive-aggressive insinuation that either I was "one of those tinfoil-hat-wearing nuts" or that some niche but very vocal groups of Western culture have pegged me as one, though I hardly took offense—"that you're like *that* dude. I'm just saying we're close to there. There's just lots of weird culty things. And even weirder sex stuff. Enough where the cops have normalized it—they don't respond fast. That's what Yvonne's boyfriend said—basically if there isn't a maniac wielding an ax, there's nothing he can do. In a professional sense, I mean."

"And . . ." Yvonne speaking. "It wasn't as though we thought our lives were in any *real* danger; it was just . . . all the moaning, the chanting—it freaked us out. It's not like a neighbor doing weird sex stuff is a danger to us."

But you didn't think you had a neighbor. Did it ever cross your mind that someone broke in?

"Sure," Massie again, "but they weren't doing a good job being stealthy, if that was the case. I just assumed someone moved in on a day I was working."

But you didn't actually think it was "weird sex stuff," either, did you?

"No, I didn't *think* it was sex stuff—but I also didn't *know* it wasn't. Though I think it's morally wrong, unless they're married, I'm also not going to be the fun police, either."

Christian?

She nods. "Catholic—you know, my parents are . . . so I guess I am, too. Isn't that kind of weird? That Catholics say they're Catholics if their parents are. Hell, I don't think I've been to church in over, I don't know . . ." She glances at Yvonne, who shrugs a *how-the-Hell-would-I-know?* shrug. "Maybe fifteen years. No confession or anything—God, that's scary."

Scary?

"I don't know," she quickly says.

"You're as Catholic as a piece of bread is Keto," says Yvonne. "You don't even believe in God; you're an Atheist—we've had heated debates about this, because you always get definitions mixed up. Remember?"

"I'm not an Atheist, I don't worship the Devil!"

Yvonne laughs at her friend, a little too harshly, and says, "My point exactly. That's not what 'Atheist' means, hon; it means you don't believe God exists."

"Really. Oh, I guess I am—*wait*. Mister, you're not going to include this in your book, are you?"

I won't (I guess that makes me a liar; but I'm keeping this part in not just for the "raw authenticity" of this conversation, but also because it bridges important themes pertaining to our protagonist Mr. Trellis and his as-of-now unseen predicament as he makes his way up the groaning stairwell of the late Rowan Esko's house). I turn to Yvonne.

Yvonne, I say, *do you know what Massie means by 'culty things'?*

"Love you, Massie, but I don't even think you know what you mean by 'culty things.' To answer your question, though, I can imagine it's kind of like in *Exodus*. When they were traveling in the desert for so long the Hebrews started to lose sight of their quest. They started creating idols and worshiping them. I think that's California."

Sounds like you're talking about "idol fixation."

"I suppose—" Yvonne starts to say.

"—but that's not what I mean about 'culty things,' Vonnie. I literally mean, like . . . I don't know . . . people who are into weird, off-putting, Zen-Jesusy-hybrid hippyish stuff; people who go into the mountains in white robes and sing hymns about the greatness of death and how life is just an illusion and we're just in *The Matrix* or something; people who take shrooms in order to pull down reality's zipper and see what's underneath; and, yeah—to come full circle—people who are into weird sex stuff, too."

I'm extrapolating that both of you might categorize the noise coming from the west-adjacent property as "culty" —hence the initial calling of your boyfriend, Jamal, on the first night, and your insistence for his coming over on the second night. Am I correct?

Massie speaking for Yvonne: "It was because of the smell and the smoke."

"Yeah," says Yvonne, "to tell the truth—and by no means do I subscribe to what I'm about to say—I was imagining some QAnon stuff. Like elites burning an infant as an offering. I mean, I'm glad it wasn't *that*— but in a weird way what we saw was . . . not worse, no, nothing's worse than a murdered baby, but *freakier*. Right?" She glances at Massie.

"Yeah, it just . . . didn't make sense. Literally. And *because* it didn't make sense, it's kind of *why* it was freaky. Because I couldn't wrap my mind around it. Couldn't imagine how the noises from the night before could have progressed into . . . what we saw . . . what the guy did to himself—and to learn from the news that he was in protective services . . . was somehow connected to that Hector Rowling thing . . . so he goes through all this trouble to hide from someone just to do *that* to himself? Didn't make sense then, doesn't make sense now, and won't make sense ever. Isn't there a famous quote about fearing the unknown?"

"The oldest and strongest emotion of mankind is fear, and the oldest and strongest kind of fear is fear of the unknown." Lovecraft.

"Yeah, I think that's the one. Then the other guy went missing, too, right?" She shakes her head. "I don't understand, Mr. Ullman—it couldn't have been suicide, but that's what the news said. Why would they *lie?*" Tears begin streaming down Massie's face; she stands up and says she "can't" and walks away. Then I turn to Yvonne.

What does Massie mean?

Yvonne looks at the ceiling. I follow her eyes' trajectory. Is she looking at the smoke alarm?

"I'm not sure what she means," she says.

I discern her distress, so I change course:

You mentioned that the night before *the discovery of his—let's say—"elaborate suicide," there had not only been moaning but also* chanting. *Can you recall any of it? Any distinct words?*

"Well, Mr. Ullman, the weird thing is . . . when I was awake with Massie . . . I didn't know . . . couldn't process it. Sounded like words, though. Yeah."

But you processed it later?

"Like we said: it took a while for us to finally fall asleep because of all the noise, and when I did finally fall asleep, somehow *it*—the chant—bled into my dreams." She noticeably shivers and spins around so abruptly that I wouldn't be surprised if she suffered whiplash the following morning. And then she stares at a sprawling spider plant in the corner of the room as if listening to it. She stays like this momentarily. Then turns. Opens her mouth and folds her arms and shivers even though it's not cold.

"It was a long, intricate dream. It stormed that night,

I remember. The trees outside the house were whapping and thrashing against one another, branches like—I don't know—primitive musical instruments. And what with the wind and the rain and the trees, I found myself in a motel or B&B on a beach. I was alone. Outside the window the moon was dull yellow and the tide was low— *too low*—and there were things washed ashore. Vague, milky outlines . . . glowing darkly in the moonlight. I know that doesn't make sense, but it was like . . . I don't know . . . they were—the silhouetted things lying on the beach—they were *eating the dark*. They were pregnant with it. That's the only way I can explain it: they were *eating the dark* and *glowing darkly*.

"But then there was a knock on my motel room door.

"And there was another noise, too—*behind* the knock. Hard to explain. Like . . . static or waves. Wind, maybe? But echoey, like listening to it down a long, long tunnel.

"'*Answer the door,*' a woman said. Husky and almost monotone. But in a *cold way*, you know? Like she was at the end of her rope. The storm and the door separating me from her muffled the voice. In the dream I was trying to think of who she was. My mother crossed my mind. I don't know why. Then she said—I *think* she said—'*and let me in.*'

"Then I thought, because I was in a motel, that it must have been room service, right? It looked like a motel room, anyway. There was a suitcase on the floor, opened, with entrails of undergarments and socks pouring out. *Men*'s underwear, *men*'s socks. But my dream-logic told me it was not necessarily that I had a boyfriend but rather—in my dream, without second-guessing it— that I was a *man*.

"So I walked across the room and opened the door. At first I actually *did* think the woman was my mom.

Just for a moment."

She pauses and looks toward the front door of her friend's condo. Is she expecting a knock?

How so? I prod.

"Even as she stood in a blot of lightless night—this was *before* she took a step inside—I could tell she was a *different kind of black.* What I mean is, I could tell she would be black even if she wasn't standing outside the illumination of the room. And she was a little overweight. That's why I thought she was my mother.

"When she walked inside the room, I could see she wasn't my mother. She was black, yes, but a *third* kind of black. And she was overweight, yes, but a *different* kind of overweight—"

I'm sorry for interrupting. But could you tell me what you mean by a 'third kind of black'?

A dark, cold beat. A draft comes through.

"Black with rot. Her voice had been calloused for the reason of her blackness and bloatedness—her *rottedness.* Her eyes explained everything to me as she walked toward me—one step, two steps—staring at me, *through me,* and she kept walking. Straight toward me. Then she fell down and she . . . I guess . . . *changed.* Into something else—you [*sic*] contacting me actually jogged my memory about what it looked like. Anyway. So her flesh fell off like she was peeling off a dress. Or a snake shedding its skin. Whatever she now was was straddling me, pressing my hands to the floor, and she opened her mouth and said something—

"Then I was in . . . some kind of void.

"For an indiscernible amount of time I was just . . . dreaming blackly. Literal black, a conscious vacuum, but then I saw light and I swam toward it. I thought it was the moon . . . then maybe a lighthouse beacon . . . but it was neither. The light was more . . . not primitive but another p-word . . . means 'ancient,' I think; it has a creepy, dehumanizing sound to it."

Primordial, I offer.

"That word. It was hovering over the black sea. It was moving, it was . . . guiding me? It terrified me."

How so?

"Because it was hungry. I knew it wanted my blood—in a way a guy might keep on blowing up my phone out of infatuation, even if I try to reject him. It was in the light's nature to want my blood. And the black around me was . . . I don't know . . . it *thrummed* with what I can only describe as *animalistic lust*; narcissism; actually, if the light I was swimming toward was the ancestor—no, the *progenitor*—of all other light to succeed it, then the abyss was the *progenitor* of narcissism, the progenitor of darkness. The First Night. I know it sounds weird but that's how I felt. And I knew it wanted to harm me, so I swam and I swam toward the hungry light even though it wanted my blood—it was the lesser of two horrors, you know? I panicked when my feet brushed up against something, but I realized it was just sand—the ground. I breathed stale air. Everywhere was black. No stars. That primordial light was gone, too, because when it made it to the beach, it just sort of lingered over a spot, illuminating what looked like a house below it. Then it blinked out, then the house lit up with that same light. Behind me there were no waves. The sea was black and as smooth as marble. When I was out of the water I noticed there was *another* light, one I hadn't noticed earlier. This one was dark."

Like a black light?

"Exactly like a black light. But it was blacker than the surrounding void I had just swum through. It was a terrible eye, I realized, atop a column of stony flesh erected somewhere farther on the beach—I couldn't tell if it was a hundred feet away, or a hundred miles. It frightened me. So I ran in the other direction, toward the lit-up house. As I neared it, I could tell it was *old*. So old that I couldn't fathom its age. And as I ran toward it, I heard plopping feet pursuing me.

"The front door was locked and boarded up, so I went around the side and tried the windows; there was one already broken, its boards laid [*sic*] on the ground next to a prybar—I didn't even think to bring it with me for protection.

"I slipped inside.

"Went upstairs.

"Found a room.

"I shut the door behind me and I heard a knock.

"It croaked out, *'Answer the call; go to Heaven.'*

"So I thought—the previous events of the dead woman and the abyss washed away, a vacant memory buried deep inside my dreaming brain—it must've been a Jehovah's Witness or something. So I went to the door and I opened it. Then I remembered everything and why I'd gone into this old house, blooming with hungry light, in the first place. Swiftly the woman walked forward. I tripped and stumbled over the suitcase. Her eyes were white and milky, her hair wet and tangled with seaweed, open wounds—bite marks—all over her bloated corpse, black with a rot assaulting my nose.

"She then fell on me. For the second time. She repeated herself, and I realized she didn't say anything about heaven. She yelled out something like, *'ANSWER THE CALL, DOG BELOW HIM—'"*

She looks at me wide-eyed; it takes me a moment to realize it's because I'm laughing.

I'm sorry. It's just—

—but I don't want to frighten her by saying that I heard a similar chant when I was a boy, on the night of my grandparents' being murdered, thus suggesting to her that her nightmare may have some . . . metaphysical merits; so I snuff it out—

—*never mind, ma'am. What happened next?*

She doesn't completely trust me. She knows I know more, and maybe my keeping the revelation to myself will, in the long run, haunt her dreamscape to unfathomably worse degrees. She composes herself and says, "Then I woke up. My body was itching all over. I looked at Massie lying on the bed next to me. At first I thought she was dead, the way her eyes were open and staring at me—"

"I asked you if you smelled that stench," says Massie, walking back to the couch, now composed. She retakes her seat next to Yvonne.

That's when you called your boyfriend, Jamal?

Yvonne nods.

You mentioned earlier that my having contacted you had "jogged your memory" regarding what the woman had "turned into." May I ask what you mean by that?

They exchange glances.

"Obviously this is my imagination," says Yvonne, then she turns around (this time in a more measured speed) and briefly surveys the spider plant before turning and facing Massie, then me, then she adds, "Because of the news and everything, and—you know—I'm just making . . . *associations* . . . that aren't . . . you know . . . *real.*"

Will you elaborate for me?

She sighs, says, "The dead woman turned into that *thing*—from the found-footage clip that went viral. They're calling it the Lagoon Monstrosity, aren't they? They're saying it's fake, though, right? Anyway. Maybe that's why I agreed to talk to you. I mean, I guess what I'm *trying* to say is . . . well, if this is *all* a hoax, then why'd they make us sign that—"

Massie elbows her; Yvonne grunts.

Massie says, "After finding the journalist over there, his lawyer made us sign an NDA—well . . . he didn't *make* us, but he gave us money. I'm assuming—because he's got Hollywood connections and friends in high places—they just didn't want people talking about the, um, suicide. Right?"

Probably, I say but I don't believe it.

I thank them for agreeing to speak with me, and after finding my way to the front door I turn and ask: *Would you two mind if I took a little trip across your backyard? I'd like to walk the same path you guys did when you went to Mr. Francis's condo.*

They don't mind.

I then walk around to Massie's backyard and absorb the Californian panorama: grass eating the sunlight and glowing a color almost too green to be green; warm breeze rustling the purple flowers of jacarandas, the vibrant leaves of Chinese pistaches; a small garden; and something else, something black and alien and weird.

I walk to Francis's city-condemned condo while keeping a close eye on this anomalous detail, which I decide on the spot to reveal to neither Massie nor Yvonne.

That there was a trail of dead spots in the grass leading from Francis's condo to Massie's, each pattern approximately the same size and the same distance apart from the preceding dead spot. I kneel down and press apart the blades of grass—gooseflesh crawling down from the nape of my neck and branching off to my hands and feet—discerning its shape.

The oval blotches of

(*a different kind of*)

blackened grass are roughly feet-shaped. These peculiar patches had emerged from the side of Francis's condo. Avoiding the nearby window of his condo by at least twelve feet, the person—likely a woman or child, considering the size of the "footprints"—must have shimmied around the house so as to avoid getting the chemical anywhere other than where she'd the black-ened-grass effect to appear. Either that or she applied the chemical to her feet only upon reaching this very spot, before walking to Massie's condo; and if the latter, then she managed, with immaculate precision, to only apply the substance to her feet and avoided getting it anywhere else, because I thoroughly check the sur-rounding area against the side of the condo for little black spots and find none. I then follow the trajectory—which, as mentioned, seems to head straight to Massie's place—stopping along the way to spread apart each blot of footprint-shaped dead grass to clarify its consistency in size, shape, and *blackness*; and now at the side of Massie's house—no window in the immediate vicinity through which the mysterious walker could climb—my eyes frantically search to see if the footprints veer left or right.

They don't.

And this near-revelation is in syncopation with a sudden, sharp yap of a dog from some faraway, gray-scaled world. I observe and process that the final foot-print is only a *partial*, as if the other half of it were *inside* the wall.

I can't wrap my head around this. That if I were to follow this trajectory of swallowed footprints *through* the wall, I wonder will it lead me directly to Massie's bed-room door? And will there be a trace of black residue approximately the size of a human knuckle?

Felix's hand comes into frame, then pushes open the same door John C. Francis had pushed open before screaming at whatever resided therein. Instead of screaming, however, Felix sort of just stands there—soaking in the

(*different kind of*)

black-spiraled walls of the room—before the reality of what it is, or what it *isn't*, comes washing over him. He backs away and bends down and gags and spits out what is related to the black designs about the room. Although he doesn't enter the room, we can clearly discern that the black about the walls is of bioorganic matter. A black mold of some sort.

Felix rushes down the stairs, trips over several boxes lining the steps, and topples over a stack of mass paperbacks—some so old and worn-out that they seemingly disintegrate before they hit the ground—all the while rapidly, breathlessly muttering to himself:

"*—John should have left—that's why they let him go—fuck shit fuck—he should have left instead of coming here but he wanted the money then he went upstairs and* *oh god oh god—he knew why they cut him they checked his blood—"*

He finds his feet and jumps down the remaining stairs, runs through the living room, and at the front he stops to cough: what comes out is black, oily goop.

Felix Trellis is dying.

But he isn't dead yet.

Three numbers (324) have been haunting him and he's determined to use them on the lighthouse safe.

AS WE STEP INTO THE final chapter, allow me to take some creative liberties in interpreting the final minutes of Felix's found footage—to really get inside his head. While it is true that the last fifteen seconds of Felix's footage were leaked from an email—and everyone and their moms have developed their own "expert opinions" on whether the underground passage was spliced footage from another location, whether the bodily dismemberment of one of the men in black (no pun intended) was special effects, or whether what the news has been calling the "Lagoon Monstrosity" was a costume, a miniature, really good CGI, or real—it is also true that the leaked footage you have undoubtedly seen is *without* the corresponding audio or other documents (which are all in *my* possession) to put what many have already seen in the appropriate context.

We are now, you and I, traversing into *Tohu wabohu*—into the **darkhouse**—down the throat and into the stomach of the swallowed town.

Into Sheol.

I'm sorry, but it had to be you.

I'd dreamt
that you'd be the one
chosen by the GREAT DOVE;
that you'd help
put an end to that Demiurge of
the Abyss and Those
Indwelt by the Void.

And he sayde: in my tribulacion I called vn to the lorde and he answered me: out of the bely of hell I cried ad thou herdest my voyce.

Jonah 2:2

THE SWALLOWED TOWN & OTHER
RABBIT HOLES YOU SHOULD AVOID
(2024), AXIOM, EXCERPT FROM THE
FINAL CHAPTER: PSYCHOABYSS

AN ARM COMES INTO FRAME (heavy breathing). The skin is dark gray (a grunt), lesions are oozing (cough cough), and the hairs on his arm are noticeably erect (*"this is it"*). A hand finds the padlock on—via fisheye lens—what looks like a coffin-sized safe (*"324 324 324 324"*). Wobbly fingers manage a 3 and a 2 and a 4 (mad mad laughter).

The padlock unlatches. Felix takes it off and opens the safe door and—

Words—*"may I help you?"*—slither into the room. He turns and sees a tall, lean figure in blue jeans and a sweater standing in the doorway (*but you're dead*, Felix might silently accuse the voyeur, yet remains silent), studying him with strange eyes before walking into the room. Shadows distort the other's face, momentarily making it elongated and semi-deformed, twisted and twitching, as if under the skin a squid were

(*fucking*)

entangled with its kin.

"I remember you from a dream," the other says, taking another step forward. "I was out there in the dark and you were looking down at me. I followed your face from the deep and the dark; it was like a lighthouse—your face was, wasn't it? I wouldn't be here if not for you and your . . . Gospel. At some point the HUNGRY LIGHT tried to heave me back into the dark; I resisted, I grabbed the ledge, and I pulled myself up just long enough to finger through the pages of your manuscript—it was these words that captivated me so:

"'*The inviolate structure: cyclopean, darkly sleeping, and always but never or sometimes encroaching like an enigmatic organism made of stone and clay or bone and blood or the residue of a god's ghost.*'"

Felix breathes heavily, garbling the audio; says nothing.

"I memorized that part, worshiped it, fantasized meeting its scribe so as to save me from the vast and empty and burning black—and now . . . now I've found you.

"Go on, turn it; you've helped me bring back my Son, ergo I'll *show* you."

The space between him and the form spun by shadow thrums with such an intensity—an energy so dark and irate and palpable, an energy with a mind, an ego—you might wonder if some of it had managed transfer itself into these very written words . . .

"You can't know until you know," says the other as if answering a question. "Hurry, before—*wait* . . ." Hector crosses the room and opens the blinds. "They followed you. But I want to show you the glory, so hurry."

He turns back around and sees that inside the safe is a small wheel-crank with a jutting-out handle.

"Turn it."

His hand finds purchase, hesitates. In the distance a car door slams shut. He turns the crank, then abruptly twists his body so he (and we) can see both the window and the other who stands in the dark of the room—perhaps in confluence with the digital limits of the button camera, perhaps not—and below a mane of thick black hair we see creaturely eyes staring back at him. Back at us. An off-putting yellow. The effigy steps further into the room's lightless corner, solid black against a milky darkness. Then nothing. Where there had been the silhouette of Hector Rowling was now empty wall, except—

Felix stumbles forward. The room is now larger: a sliding door, previously camouflaged with the rest of the wall, has slid into its pocket, revealing to us—as Felix enters, looking left then right—a passage running the length of the room. It dead-ends at the hallway to his left. But to his right . . . a floor hatch, a cast-iron lid propped open . . . then footfalls and moaning floorboards . . .

Panicking, cursing.

"They *want to see as much as you do, Hushed Oracle. Come down below and see.*"

Felix finds a ladder rung and climbs down the throat . . .

. . . THE VIDEO BECOMES A SLUDGE of black blacks and gray grays. As the same *morbus* that had killed my parents slowly and effectively eats away his mind—as the same order of black-van occupants who had killed my grandparents pursue him—perhaps he sees, in the vicinity of the ladder rungs in the low-light of the abyss-descending shaft—as he grunts, as he screams, as he cries, as he prays—the oracular *nightfish* in their vivid, quantifiable forms, as they swim through dimensional veils. Perhaps carpeting the

(*throat*)

suffocatingly close walls of the shaft are heaps upon heaps of moldering sea matter composed of calcified bones bleeding through the putrid and oozing scales or skin, or stone and clay, or bone and blood, or the residue of some strange god's ghost. Perhaps he truly sees, perhaps he truly doesn't. And approximately one minute and fifteen seconds before we witness what the denizens of pop culture have coined the "Lagoon Monstrosity," Felix Trellis says, "*. . . an amalgamation—a convergence—of everythingness. Of*"

(*a gagging sound; audio levels spike; a fleck of subterranean illume in the opaque, grainy muck*)

"*nothing. Just a void. An oblivion. A beacon . . .*"

One imagines, in the thick darkness, a lingering malarial-tinged stench—pungent, stomach-churning, *vexatious*—saturating this world of Night.

Footfalls.

At this point it's clear that Felix Trellis has reached the bottom of the shaft, has made contact with the floor. Clicks and clacks and the clattering of loose stone and shells (*or bones*). Squelching of damp earth or sand and splish-splashing of puddles of water. And do we hear a wobbling low wind, *conchlike*, coming from the source of the weird shimmer of what may be—no, *what certainly is*—water-reflected moonlight bleeding

("*. . . a reliquary—for not only the things—vacuous emissaries—or thing—the Great Dove/God's Hand—in the Void but the essence of vacuity Itself, the soul of Black Itself . . .*")

around the tunnel's bend. About the earthy serpent's gloomy insides—the throat leading into the esophagus leading into the stomach—are jutting-out pyrgoidal shapes.[26]

Camera shaking; wheezing; coughing. A horrid painting of griseous obscurities as we move closer to the moony glow. A squawking—of birds or something else: we can't know for certain—raptorial and ravenous. The farther light falters and is suddenly occulted. *Eclipsed.* Felix breathes in deeply and exhales and trips and stands up and narrates to us as he goes deeper and deeper into the heart of all things[27]:

"A pearlescent shaft.

"A bone.

"Human.

---

[26] While most viewers deemed the leaked footage faux in nature upon its initial release—thus neglecting to apply critical thinking to the miscellaneous details (i.e., the chirping of the "birds"; the species of large, star-shaped mushrooms scattered about the floor [difficult to make out unless digitally enhanced]; and the "spires" upon the walls and ceiling)—those who did take the footage seriously deduced these shapes to be mere mineral buildups. However, when digitally enhanced, one can discern holes—*tunnels*—at the tips of what Dr. Procyzardo of Harvard identified as "a cluster of nests."

[27] Since the button camera has shifted to a permanent upward tilt—likely due to Felix's tumbling—it's difficult to know whether he's speaking nonsensically or truly observing these things on the ground.

"A femur.

"Pale, rotted jack-o-lantern. Eyes gaping and black and homes to abyss-dwelling, post-mortem, morbid parasites—Loligo and Decapods—and fist-sized germs and algae and—and—viruses—oh fuck—reality-viruses, *meta*-viruses."

He starts laughing—and in what may be a passable David Attenborough impersonation:

"The specimen Felix Trellis—synaptic madness crippling his psyche, casting it into an atemporal mush, a psychoabyss (hey everyone"—now in a normal voice—"assuming this footage makes it through these walls and gets uploaded to the cloud, assuming I haven't stumbled into the Solemnity of Dag Elohim instead of the Festival of the Fish—what I mean is: *into another reality*, like . . . like some multiversal bullshit, you know?—so, yeah, and if someone writes a book [yeah, I'm talking to you, Wayward Ron], I think that would be a great title for this chapter: *Psychoabyss*—anyway, where was I?)"; and back to Attenborough:

"The specimen has stilts for legs holding up a hundred and fifty pounds of disease-riddled meat but still he walks toward the thing which obstructs the light source ahead of him.

"'Hey, you!' Felix called out stupidly to Hector Rowling's meatsuit as he navigated the bend in the tunnel, revealing about the floor—now flooded in a most feverish, dreamy moonlight—niveous powder: probably Matanah Ne'evah shit," Felix calls out stupidly to the humanoid silhouette as he navigates the bend in the tunnel. Where the other stands, two eyes—yellow and catlike—blink toward us in the murk.

And the shape—sounding *mostly* like Hector Rowling—groggily says, "Almost home now, Hushed Oracle.

By Father *Shachor*[28] be healed. Eat it *all* away He will."
"Eat what away?" His words are drunkenly slurred.
"*Who* are you?"
Felix doesn't answer.
"*What* are you?"
"Human?"
"Are you?"
"Aren't I?"
"*When* are you?"
Felix takes a step forward so as to better see the

---

[28] שָׁחוֹר is Hebrew for "black." It's pronounced "shachor." We also see in the journals of the first settlers that more than six of them had dreams of a black silhouette, one shaped like a shark or an orca, and that each of these dreamers had felt a sense of rage and intent-to-do-violence in its demeanor (one journal entry had called it an "oily attitude"). In fact, in the several preserved journals you can find testimony of Eberlein Grayson—well-versed in Hebrew, for, as you may recall, he'd been a Rabbi prior to his Christian conversion—telling three of these dream-sufferers that the black silhouette was "as harmless as a drunk father punching walls." It is therefore easy to deduce that he'd used the Hebrew word for "black" at some point during their conversations and, eventually, the name "Father Shachor" stuck. Plus, it seems like a common motif for Church of the Fish members—as is the case with "Dag Elohim," which means "Fish of God"—to spell out in English the pronunciation of Hebrew words.

other.

"Stop"—and he stops. "*Where* are you?"

"Are you . . . interviewing *me?*"

"No," says the other. "But this is *your* last chance to interview *me.* Yuri mentioned you wanted to ask me questions. I refused. But considering where I'm at, and what you've done, and what's about to be done, I don't see how it'll hurt." Hector takes a step toward us, eyes momentarily taking on a radioactive greenish hue. The strange color pierces the dark. Pierces me and my future and my past—my boyhood—and, as he takes one more step closer, his eyes blink out. They're snuffed like a thumb and forefinger pinching a flame. Nothing. And the silhouette, blockish and blackish, obsequiously amalgams to the surrounding darkness. There's a snaky black hole standing there.

As I wrote that most recent passage, I noticed a coldness gathering in my den. It seems unnatural, and I can't seem to get warm.

Would you call me a *superstitious old man* if I were to tell you I feared that Father Shachor is trying to stop me? Stop me from finishing this tale?

So let me pause.

Pause the footage. Pause the writing.

Let the cursor blink—fade in and out. In and out.

Right here.

Just for a little while as I compose myself.

I'm back.

I realize I have a carnal need for answers. So I look

back at the paused pixelated footage. I stabilize my nerves as I peer into blackness. Into *abyss*. Nietzsche comes to mind. A quote of his about staring too deeply into it.

There's no monster. Yet. The inexplainable uncanniness feels like evidence of there being an *off-screen wrongness* (looking over my shoulder I half expect a man-shaped shadow with yellow or green eyes staring at me from the darkened hallway through my cracked open office door—but there's nothing, only a gap of black . . . but what if I were to stare long enough . . . ?); and what if that very abstract forbiddingness is what actually *lures* the monster?

So, yes . . . the cold floor . . . and I think maybe I'm having the opposite of a waking nightmare as I write these final words. Maybe I'm awake but also dreaming, in a state of déjà vu (have I relived this moment? Have *you* relived this moment? Have we engaged in this abyssal interview for eternity? *Beyond* eternity?); so I get up and put on my slippers and dreamwalk to the window looking out over the front yard and see what I first think is—what my upper-middle-age brain deciphers as—a big black shark lying still, very very still, on my driveway. Big dull eyes staring at me. Challenging me—to do what? To finish writing this book? To use Felix Trellis as an avatar to interview Hector Rowling? Do I rewrite history? Or do I relay to you exactly what occurs in the email-received footage and audio?

I'll let you decipher.

And let me tell you this: no grin so white has ever shone so dark. So *big*. Almost humanlike but certainly sentient. Then it swims or slithers away wraithlike down my short and straight driveway, between my neighbors' houses, to the city beyond, and then it—if not the Abyss itself (i.e., Father Shachor), certainly one of its harrowing offspring—just . . . vanishes.

When I step back to my desk and first look at one monitor where my Microsoft Word file is open (THE SWALLOWED TOWN grins whitely and darkly across the surrounding darkness of the title bar) and the cursor is fading in and out of existence, in and out, and in . . . when I look at the other monitor where I'd paused the footage, where there's indistinct black about indistinct black, where I'm a ten-year-old boy looking out a window . . . I think I see those eyes again, and a thin line of a mouth—not human, not Hector Rowling's mouth, no. I see two pectoral fins on either side and a dorsal atop, and I know what this brood, this DWELLER OF THE ABYSS, actually is. I know this isn't my imagination; it never was. I know Felix had seen and felt a very similar presence. And I finally have a face to the name, a fleshly, temporal face for

(*the shark took their heads*)

the *darkness*:

What I had said to the dispatch operator—"the shark took their heads"—after I'd seen what I'd seen (via some unconscious survival mechanism I threw away the macabre memory's key, and with a stubborn zeal I've neither accepted therapy nor hypnosis to draw out that palpable darkness) as a young boy on the night of my grandparents' murders in Charlotte, Michigan, never made sense to me until now.

The shark is Dag Elohim.

Dag Elohim is the Fish of God.

The Fish of God is Father Shachor . . .

. . . and Father Shachor—the black thing that has been dwelling in my dreams, that had plagued the minds of John C. Francis and Felix Trellis, too—is what it is, and is what it eats . . .

. . . darkness.

Black.
Void.
Lonesomeness.
Depression.
Disease.
Death.
Mold . . .

. . . a forever blinking cursor; an unfinished manuscript; aborted dreams; unreachable vistas; a low wind, *conchlike,* sifting from the gap under a closed door like groping fingertips . . . or a fin belonging to the original *Orcinus Orca*: no, the primordial progenitor, the apotheosis of all the emissaries of Sheol . . .

. . . IT'S BEEN MONTHS SINCE I'VE written. I thought maybe I would conclude *The Swallowed Town* in opaque mystery, however frustrating it may be to the reader, and just chalk it up to *artistic decisions.* Perhaps to claim that the mystery is greater than the answers, the journey more important than the end, you get the idea.

Or—the high-road reason, the domineering keeper of knowledge—I might have told myself I was actually *protecting* the reader; that there were some things better not knowing for their (I suppose *your*) own safety.

But I'm neither so purposefully and daringly artistic enough to end with a cliffhanger, nor am I righteous enough to protect you from this outer darkness pervading from all around, boiling us to death like lobsters—only it takes many and many more decades for the meal to be fully cooked and for us to be prepared on a deep rectangular dish, where placed atop us for taste is a lid and flowers and dirt and a slab of mineral—because I can't protect you from IT; because Father Shachor, or one of its kinfolks, will find us all in the end.

So let's meet it on our own terms.
Let's go back to the tunnel of the darkhouse.
Let's press play.
Let's finish our interview.

I'M BACK AGAIN. My editor told me to get rid of this part here (as well as much of what you've read prior), but I feel compelled to communicate to you, Dear Reader, how much I'm dragging my feet. How does one describe the indescribable? And what is describable is, to put it mildly, unpleasantly gruesome.

Reader discretion is advised—there's going to be some *bur-oo-tull dis-mem-bur-ment*.

*"THIS IS ONLY **MY** DREAM."*

(mild static)

"What do you mean, Mr. Rowling? Are you saying I'm in your dream? Like a . . . passenger?"

"I mean what I mean. You've got questions but you don't have much time . . ." As he pauses, we hear footfalls, shouting, and . . . whispers. *"And I know you want me to confess my innocence. That perhaps I did not kill the family and could not stop the Guardians from carrying out their ritual. Perhaps it was a necessary correction, you see; rectifying the misalignment caused by Uncle Bill. Remember Uncle Bill? Running from responsibility, running from Dag Elohim. Or perhaps they were let in, let in to behead the mother; watched when they did that to the sister and the father, oh blessed be **MY** name—"*

((static ramps up scratchier angrier deeper darker))

"—but you did not kill your family . . . physically, I mean . . . that's what I want to ask."

"—that's not what I'm saying and that's not what you're asking, Hushed Oracle. There's a reason why Uncle Bill committed suicide, being the oldest male, succeeding his father. Wouldn't be here if he hadn't taken those pills. It would be one of his sons."

"What do you mean?"

"The Keeper."
"The Lighthouse Keeper?"
Harsh
(((whispers)))
white noise.
"There's nothing light about this place. But none of that's true, anyway. About innocence and misalignments and rituals. Yuri told it straight, Mr. Trellis. You sang our ballad, the world listened, and poor Hector Rowling was freed. Then he tried to really free himself from the top of an overpass. But he wasn't free, not really; are any of us? The Dark—the Rot—had already taken root"—a sniffing
((((. . . sun flickers
the stars o the stars blink
blink out
blink in then out
fade fast
retract
fade forever
rescind . . .))))
sound—"as I think you know all about"—now a
(((((. . . forlorn thing
an impassive watcher
a formless creature drenched in lonesomeness
despite the forever-company of its contorted
    children
of indifference
despite the sobbing of their suffering and pleading
    for mercy
for light
I watch in discombobulated terror as its great
    appendage swings back and forth like a blind
        idiot . . .)))))
*chuckle—"and the Guardians, those fools, trying to contain **ME**! Even the Company, while they don't believe*

in **ME**, they at least understand the importance of **ME**."
  ((((laughter))))
  "Who are the Guardians? What Company?"
  "They're coming right now."
  "Who is?"
  (((silence)))
  "If you did your job you would already know."
  "The tribe? The ones who lived here when the settlers came?"
  ((silence))
  "And the company. Cr███ll?"
  (silence)
  "If yes, then why? If no, then who?"
  Silence and then:
  "The better questions, Trellis, are 'why did they want Hector Rowling to come back home?' and 'who helped you find evidence of his innocence?' and 'why did he jump off an overpass?' and 'why did his uncle Bill Rowling take too many pills?' and 'why were the Guardians trying to open the safe and come down here and stare into the Formless Brine? To worship it, to weaponize it, to contain it, or to destroy it?'"
  "You're not Hector Rowling?"
  Silence.
  "Who are you?"
  Silence and then:
  "That which stares back."
  Silence and then:
  A burst of fussy white noise, a high wind
  ((((((hurricanelike))))))
  End of file.

Reaction guest: *Hello, I'm Michael Farmauser. I'm a professional digital and practical effects artist. Today I'll be looking at the alleged found footage from last year's Pulitzer Prize winner—and, I guess, ironic cultural icon because of all that . . . stuff that happened to him. Crazy year for that fella; and I only hope this is fake because [indecipherable muttering]. I mean, c'mon, it's gotta be fake, right? Monsters? Hey, I got an idea—maybe it was a pilot from that Tic Tac UFO—or UAP, EAP, whatever they're called now—*

So, yeah. We'll be watching the footage and I'll give my reactions. I guess it's not a very long video. And no, I haven't actually watched it yet. I've only seen the thumbnails circulating on YouTube and TikTok, and assume it's AI-generated—because all thumbnails are AI-generated these days, aren't they? Because, you know— Bigfoot, Loch Ness, UAPs, the Rake, Slender Man— they're all blurry, so the thumbnail can't be a screenshot from the actual *video. A real screenshot would probably be just a black blur or something if I had my guess; but let's see what the—*

Producer: *It's an actual screenshot. They enhanced it*

though. Popped the saturation and vibrancy. It's surprisingly pretty good footage. Grainy but good. Which is why there's so much controversy. I guess that off-brand Alex Jones guy—Wayward Whatever-His-Name-Is—has the [air quotes] full video. He's writing—or wrote—a book on it.

Reaction guest: *No [duck sound]. Well, let's watch this and I'll tell you guys if it's CGI, practical effects—good or bad—or AI-generated. [a beat] Okay, black screen. Fuzzy. What's that? Oh, his arm. What is this? Go Pro? [video pauses]*

Producer: *Some kind of button camera. Footage routinely uploaded to cloud. That's how it was recovered. It was sent to Trellis's acquaintance who had instructions to send it to some blogger who then sent it to Wayward Ron.*

Reaction guest: *Very convenient, but okay. [video resumes] Grainy footage, of course. It's to be expected even if the button camera is 1080p. Cameras that are also good in low light are really expensive. Okay, so our protagonist—Felix Trellis, allegedly—is running. There's a glow. What is that? Water? Is this a cave or something? Is the water glowing? Interesting effect. And now Trellis is staring at the weirdly glowing water. Some kind of well or spring—I'm assuming it goes to the ocean, considering this is under a lighthouse. It's got a dull lunar quality, if that makes sense. Is there anything in the water? There's no audio. I imagine the button camera he bought sacrificed audio for slightly better image processing. There's definitely something in the water. [video pauses]*

Producer: *The internet folk have enhanced it as well as possible. Apparently what you're looking at are . . . ma-*

rine organisms. *Some are calling them [air quotes] glob-sters. But they're likely the same organisms that show up on that particular coast during that particular time of year. The* Festival of the Fish. *The locals call them* Sea Manna. *That's* likely *what you're looking at—*

Other producer: *—which throws another wrench in the whole proving it as a fake video. The Sea Manna species is protected under some kind of religious rights law, so anyone caught stealing one will face a hefty fine—not to mention that the locals themselves are pretty stringent about tourists taking any that wash ashore. They're very . . . religious about it.*

Producer: *There are also conspiracy theories that the local government couldn't care less about the religious stuff—that the Sea Manna are actually just highly toxic. Like I said: just a theory. But the tin-foil camps seem to be polarizingly divided between a Lovecraftian/Occult origin and a* Resident Evil-*esque public safety matter.* AKA, *it either being a "supernatural" curse or a naturalistic biohazard.*

Reaction guest: *I apparently should have done my homework. [video resumes] Yep, still staring at the underground spring. And, oh [duck sound], there's the, uh, Lagoon Monstrosity. It's picking up a guy in a black trench coat, black rubber gloves, black boots, black gasmask. [duck sound, duck sound, duck sound, video pauses] I mean, c'mon, someone had to have doctored this, right? So you can see next to the webbed feet of the Lagoon Monstrosity that there's a pile of clothes and maybe . . . skin? Human hair, too? Hard to tell. And even though there isn't a lot of light, you can clearly see a human face in that heap. Black vacant eyes. Reminds me of some-*

thing Rob Zombie would do. The clear indication is that the thing discarded its human meat suit. I mean—[duck sound] Okay. [video resumes] Okay, it's pulling pulling pulling—arm snaps off. That's pretty realistic because it's not a clean rip. You can see it has pulled even further until the sleeve of the trench coat rips. And, okay, realistic blood—not too bright, definitely not digital. Nice. Or not nice, I guess, considering . . . [video pauses] There must be a tube somewhere in there, must be a motor pumping out blood, because there's enough clothing to conceal the bag of fake blood.

[video resumes]

We've got Dude Number Two swinging a . . . what is that, a tomahawk ax? Tries putting his friend out of his misery, gets him in the neck. But the Lagoon Monstrosity is just not having it.

A tail or—oh, okay—a tentacle—of course it's a tentacle—comes whipping out from its back-area. Dude Number Two falls backward into the darkness. The Monstrosity then grips his neck wound, pulls apart, and—

[camera tilts upward, water, end of video]

No wonder the news doesn't play the whole video. That was graphic to say the least.

Producer: *Overall opinion?*

Reaction guest: *[a beat, laughter, seriousness] What I can say is this: if it is CGI, then it's the greatest CGI I've ever seen. Therefore it's not; can't be; no; you can tell by how the thing's skin glistens with blood and other . . . bodily fluids . . . and with just its general movements. There seems to be no indication of CGI. It's all practical effects. You've just got really high-end animatronics, especially considering the motion of the appendage knocking back Dude Number Two. Or . . .*

[a beat]

Producer: *Or what?*

Reaction guest: *Or it wasn't animatronics, if you catch my drift. But then you'd have to talk to a biologist about that, not me. Or [laughs] a demonologist.*

Producer: *You think it's real?*

Reaction guest: *I hope it's not real. But [duck sound], if whoever did this decides to get into filmmaking—mainstream filmmaking, I mean—then I might be out of a job. It's really, really good animatronics. Very lifelike. And I'll say it again: definitely not CGI. But I'm a little disturbed by something else. Can you go back?*

[**Producer** rewinds]

Reaction guest: *Stop. Can you play this in slow motion? Okay, you see when the Lagoon Monstrosity knocks Dude Number Two into that shadowy area? There. Pause. He clearly strikes the wall, slides down, and you see his legs splayed out. I haven't heard anybody talk about this yet, so if this is fake then I don't see why they tried so hard to conceal this really good, really nuanced effect.*

Other producer: *I think I see what you're talking about.*

Producer: *What?*

Other producer: *On the floor, look. The shadow.*

Producer: *Isn't that just a shadow?*

Reaction guest: *Well, look. It's, I guess, disembodied; not cast by Felix Trellis—the cameraman—and it's not cast by the Lagoon Monstrosity. Play it as slow as possible. [slow motion] It looks like a big—*

Producer: *—[duck sound] shark. Looks like it's swimming—darting across the ground—and—*
[duck sound]

Reaction guest: *Yep. That shadow seems to originate from the Lagoon Monstrosity, zips across the cavern floor, seems to camouflage itself with the pitch-black corner, and then you can see Dude Number Two getting yeeted into it, like he's pulled by a cord—yanked right off the ground. Two seconds later, you can see bottom half of his body fall out of corner. [duck sound] Just look at that blood gushing out. [duck sound]*

Producer: *Are you sure it's not CGI?*

Reaction guest: *[a long beat]. Yeah. I'm sure. [another beat] It's as if that shark-shaped shadow bit right through him.*

I sit here on most nights, just before sunset, especially around the time of the Festival. *The magic hour*, they call it; and if you're a ritualistic watcher of the sun during this time of day, wherever you may be on the third planet from the sun, you'll know why it's *magic*—not just for film or photography, but for the soul: a resetting of one's psychic equilibrium, perhaps. On my back patio, I sit. I may not have a vantage of the ███████ Ocean, but I can at least see the ancient trees whose great branches shade the sand that rims it. A pipe in my mouth, I sit. A ritualistically brought-along-but-never-opened novel— sometimes Faulkner, McCarthy, maybe Dickens, or Dostoevsky—I sit, I watch the great orb sink, and I feel the wind ruffle my last-remaining strands of gray hair. Sometimes, during this *hour of magic*, as I sit here and stare and smoke and think, especially around the time of the Festival, I wonder what it's like living in the eye of the storm.

This once quaint and rustic town nestles against the usually-calm waters of the ████████; chock-full of sea-breeze-corroded, sun-beaten, *homely* homes—upon which you wouldn't think twice about gazing while passing through town—now have about them, through my forevermore tainted eyes, an occult moaning against the wind, esoteric and eldritch, where, if you watch closely, very closely and intently, you can see about their contours, especially against the rising or setting sun—and even *more* especially around the time of the Festival—an insane sagging, fluctuating, *chanting*, not with profound age or advanced decay or with the will of the seaborn squall . . . but something else entirely. Something unknowable.

Lucky me to live outside city limits. Also lucky me to have made a living—albeit not a lavish one—working at home.

When I was a younger man, I'd take maybe five- or six-mile walks into town via the beach (there's a little trail at the edge of my property that cuts straight to the sea) and I'd pass the area where, allegedly, ██████'s founding fathers and mothers had set up camp and starved until the GREAT DOVE clawed and brought up into the sky Jonah's Fish and dug its talons into its guts to feed the desperate, starving settlers; I'd pass the Great Fast memorial, down Main Street, where I'd then take a right to stare upon the still-standing-but-heavily-modernized Church of the Fish (I'd pass gaggles of aimless, parentless, besmirched children—spiritually summoned specters from a long-lost era—wearing wood-carved fish faces, orbitual eyes charcoal-black and eerily blank, lips red as if blood-stained); then the lighthouse, where I'd contemplate the existential terror of degeneration and mortality, and the transcendent beauty of birth and unreachable vistas. But the former, like a brutal shark, would always swallow the latter, leaving behind a tainted psychic residue. Something about the lighthouse and the town below always felt off, about the buildings, too . . . and the air: a *stench* of sulfur and brine and rot—of some long-dead deep-sea Leviathan's carcass, which had marinated the town's bones and all: a fermentation of its soul—thus shaping an unsettling *genius loci* that transcends time and space—seems to simultaneously and paradoxically trickle backward and forward in time.

As an older man, especially after reading Ron Ullman Junior's sixth novel, *The Swallowed Town & Other Rabbit Holes You Should Avoid*, I walk considerably less distance. I also walk the other direction.

At the moment I sit.

I watch.

I smoke.

I wait.

Now I write.

I don't know what to make of this town and its history, but my eyes are now open enough to know that there's something *not quite right*. Though they've always been present (in fact, ever since I've been a boy), I'm *more* aware of C██████l's activity, especially around the time of the Festival; *more* aware of how *strange* the members of the Church of the Fish are, especially around the time of the Festival, especially after the consumption of the *Sea Manna*—via Unity of the Fish Day, which is the first day of their washing ashore; and of how—on some nights around the *magic hour*, especially around the time of the Festival, beyond the palm trees lining my property to the south—I can hear a brood of singing cicadas. Except there are no cicadas in the ocean and they're not singing, whatever they are—they're worshiping; they're joyfully suffering; they're waiting . . .

I had a dream a few months back.

I was at the rim of a chasm deep in the ocean.

There was an old manuscript, somehow undamaged by the sea or the ocean's depth where it lay. From the dark beyond I heard the worshipful chant of those aforementioned cicadas. But I could only make out the opaque forms of their long-leggedness, their suffering eyes (round and black like those Fish Festival masks), their whimpering maws (red with blood). I had some psychotic, hypnotic, or primal urge to read from the manuscript despite a sense of danger from the Brood of Things around me that kept to the darkness, and of something in the chasm beyond where the manuscript lay, in a deeper sort of darkness—the ABYSS itself; but before I could make it to the manuscript, I woke up.

The following day—on a whim and if for no other reason than to decimate his work the same way I'd slaughtered his grandfather's books, not to mention his own previous five novels—I read Ullman's *The Swallowed Town & Other Rabbit Holes You Should Avoid*. Then I got to the part about Felix's dreams about the manuscript near the chasm . . .

I don't know what happened to Felix Trellis, nor do I know why John R. Francis burned himself alive, nor if the "Lagoon Monstrosity" is real or doctored, but I believe *something* happened—something I can't explain rationally, something that slinks into the realm of the paranormal or supernatural or extracosmic—because we were both passengers in the same "dream-place." I neither understand what it means, nor how it connects with the Church of the Fish and the enigmatic presence of the pharmaceutical conglomerate C███████l, nor why law enforcement usually find Native American corpses— usually male—around the ████████ area (though friends and family never report them missing, and they are rarely identified). There must be some strange overlap, some ominous association, some deeper connotation. But for all I don't know and don't understand, I believe there are others—haunting the streets of ████ ████—who, too, dream of a town (*our* town) swallowed by darkness; and of the ABYSS beyond; and of a low wind—what sounds like a brood of cicadas—rising from the sea. *Especially* around the time of the Festival.

—Ralph Margo Stovington
December 15th, 2024

[Un]Found Footage

Our prophet lies on monochrome sand, facedown. We watch him at a comfortable distance—close enough to see what looks like chemical burns covering his exposed gray-black flesh, but far enough and perhaps quiet enough *where he doesn't hear us.* Despite his skin's grotesqueness, his clothes and shoes are untarnished save for their drenched appearance and the tangled imbroglio of his shirt.

Fingers squeeze sand, sifts through fingers.

Coughs.

Thrashes.

Spins around and lies on his back. He now sees an organism—what appears to be a great ancestor to the modern crab—which has attached itself to his flesh through his ripped-open shirt. Screaming, he yanks at the organism. Its legs thrash about as it pulls out an unnaturally long proboscis from his sternum. Black ooze dribbles down. The man shoves the organism away. It lands on its back, spasms, rights itself, and absconds into—as we pan up, and quite smoothly to boot—a crystal-clear sea.

He pants.

Then coughs.

Then coughs up black.

Then screams, then cries, then moans, then touches

his chest—his sternum—then winces.

Then gingerly places forefinger and thumb to his flesh and winces again and pulls out what you might think is a ██████████████████████ but isn't even in the same ball-park of species.

Shh.

He mustn't hear us. Watch this. Watch the shoreline and beyond and see the moon in the sky, too huge, stars too low. Watch that which dances in the superblack between the glittering ghosts in the celestial canopy. Watch as he knows where he is—home, finally home—and how his posture slackens at the realization that this is not quite a dream. Or perhaps that it's the FINAL DREAM.

More of those broods of not-crabs clatter about the beach.

The Children of Father Shachor, of Dag Elohim—and not just the great- but the great-great-great-grandchildren of the LONESOME GREAT DREAMER—have found their new prophet to finish writing the MANUSCRIPT, to rekindle the ███ of the **darkhouse**.

He sees this. Their zealous onslaught emerging from the endless sea. Their clattering claws. Their too-long legs. Their almost-human lips and the dead stars of their hollowed eyes inside elongated faces like rotted dog heads. Their familiar voices like low winds, their terrible, staticky elevator music like singing cicadas.

He sees, too, amid the sea abounding with life, the writhings of great and unknowable leviathans. He backs away from this unreachable vista, pulls out a thin, black rectangle and curses ███

(not that ██ *can hear you anyway, mayhap we think, mayhap we say)*

for its uselessness here—and then, almost instantaneously, it's full dark.

The new prophet is quick-witted enough, however, to

summon a source of light from his otherwise useless black rectangle.

We can't make out much, other than his starlit silhouette against the hungry sea and the swinging-back-and-forth torch giving him and his surroundings some definition, albeit milky and distorted.

He stops running. He must see us because he screams. Only briefly. Then changes trajectory, jumps over one of the not-crabs, screams again as a great claw snaps at him, tears a thread of his jeans, of his flesh. Blood spews out hissing against cold sand. A few of the not-crabs start ravenously lapping it off the ground—blood and sand and all—as the others follow the new prophet at a steady gait to the Inviolate Structure, which may look to him like an old beach house where a dying yellow-white glow whispers from its window.

The sound of their voices, of their ballad, is like a low wind, conchlike.

"THERE'S NO HOPE LEFT" is the last thing he says—to the black rectangle? we wonder—on the other side of the door, and we knock on it.

The prophet gasps, something clatters, and the mold of silence festers and grows.

"Answer the call," we say—to which this time the prophet doesn't gasp, only pretends to be void.

Knocking, repeating our message—over and over and over again we do this—hearing only his muted breathwork and the low bum-bum, bum-bum, bum bum of a darkly wallowing heart. But eventually the deep keys of a black organ murmur across the floor; its five-toed musicians take their summoning place before the door, where through the sill prophesy two pools of shadow—spilt ink thirsty for its quill. Then the knob begins to turn.

Acknowledgments

First and foremost, I'd like to thank Kristina Osborn for taking a chance on *The Swallowed Town*. Truborn Press may specialize in weird horror, but I sometimes wonder if maybe this novel tested the limits. If it veered a little *too* far into the strange, the off-beat, the ambiguous—thank you taking a chance.

William Sterling, who navigated this book's winding sentences, archaic vocabulary, eccentric humor, and my Frankensteinian McCarthy-King-Lovecraft punctuation experiments—I am truly grateful for your help, and I am sorry for the grammatical torture I've put you through.

To Matthew M. Bartlett, Zack Graham, Aleco Julius, Michael Wehunt, Derek Austin Johnson, Pedro Iniguez, Nick Botic, Felix Blackwell, and Adam Nevill—thank you for your encouragement and moral support along the way.

I would also like to extend heartfelt thanks to Ivy Grimes, Corey Farrenkopf, Andrew Najberg, Richard Beauchamp, Elford Alley, Charlotte Dune, and Tobin Elliott for their generous blurbs and kind words.

To Matt Cardin—thank you for inspiring the philosophical framework that shaped this novel's deeper themes. Your work challenged me to think more critically and ambitiously.

And finally, thank you to everyone who helped proofread the manuscript. Milt Theodossiou, in particular—he's a reading machine, and I'm not entirely convinced he's human. Your sharp eyes and thoughtful feedback were instrumental in shaping this book into its final form.

Please follow me on Instagram, Threads, and X; my handle on all three is **@CFPage_Author**. I'm also **Jordan CF Page** on Facebook—feel free to send me a friend request.

Since I do not yet have literary representation, I'm relying heavily on word of mouth and reviews. Amazon, Goodreads, and Books of Horror (a Facebook group— you should join it if you haven't already) are the best places . . . at least, at the time of my writing this (7/11/25). Reviews—good, bad, and ugly—especially on Amazon—are the lifeblood of any indie author's career, so I can't stress enough how much it helps if you find some time to write up a couple of sentences after finishing *The Swallowed Town.*

The world of this novel—imbued with what I call the Anterior Mythos, which is something I've been working on for the better part of a decade—also connects with my previous two published works: a novel called *Native Fear* (Jordan Peele's *Get Out* meets John Carpenter's *The Thing*) and a collection called *Orphans of the Atercosm (Side A)* . . . Side A?! Whoa, dude. *The Swallowed Town* is Side B.

We want to thank our readers for their support and enthusiasm. Your passion for stories fuels our commitment to bring you the horror that is strange and horrifying in the best of ways.

We appreciate any and all reviews, so help us out by leaving your thoughts online.

Thank you again for spending your time with us and remember to...

Follow us everywhere: @trubornpress
Subscribe to our newsletter today!
www.trubornpress.com